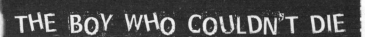

THE BOY WHO COULDN'T DIE

Other books by William Sleator

NOVELS
Blackbriar
House of Stairs
Into the Dream
The Green Futures of Tycho
Fingers
Interstellar Pig
Singularity
The Boy Who Reversed Himself
The Duplicate
Strange Attractors
The Spirit House
Others See Us
Dangerous Wishes
The Night the Heads Came
The Beasties
The Boxes
Rewind
Bolzmon!
Marco's Millions
Parasite Pig
The Last Universe

BOOKS FOR YOUNGER READERS
The Angry Moon
Among the Dolls
Once, Said Darlene
That's Silly

MEMOIR
Oddballs

THE BOY WHO COULDN'T DIE

William Sleator

Amulet Books
New York

Library of Congress Cataloging-in-Publication Data: Sleator, William.
The boy who couldn't die / William Sleator.
p. cm.
Summary: When his best friend dies in a plane crash, sixteen-year-old Ken
has a ritual performed that will make him invulnerable, but soon learns that
he had good reason to be suspicious of the woman he paid to lock his soul away.
hardcover ISBN 0-8109-4824-9
paperback ISBN 0-8109-8790-2
[1. Immortality—Fiction. 2. Zombies—Fiction. 3. Supernatural—Fiction.]
I. Title: Boy who could not die. II. Title.

PZ7.S6313Bne 2004
[Fic]—dc22
2003022382

Printed and bound in Canada
10 9 8 7 6 5 4 3 2

Design: Interrobang Design Studio

AMULET

Published in 2005 by
Amulet Books, a division of
Harry N. Abrams, Inc.
100 Fifth Avenue
New York, NY 10011
www.abramsbooks.com

Abrams is a subsidary of

LA MARTINIÈRE
GROUPE

For Susan Van Metre,
my editor,
who knows how to wring it out of me

THE BOY WHO COULDN'T DIE

"You're sure you want to do this, now?" the middle-aged woman said in her heavy New Yawk accent, sitting across the cluttered room from me in a black leather chair. The only light came from a floor lamp next to her.

She was irritating. "Would I go to all the trouble to get here if I wasn't sure?" I asked her.

She shifted in her chair. The shorts she was wearing were much too small for someone her age, showing her flabby thighs. Her carefully styled blonde hair was dyed. "No snappy wisecracks, please," she said. "Just an honest answer." She folded her arms across her chest. "Once it is done, it's not easy going back. Never. And I'm not accustomed to dealing with uppity teenagers."

I sighed. I had to treat this old biddy right. There was no other way. "Yeah, okay," I said. "But I really do want to do it. And I have the money."

"You have to consider all the consequences," she said slowly. "You can't just change your mind and unlock your soul from its hiding place, like that." She snapped her fingers, long nails flashing. "Someday you may find yourself in a situation where you don't *want* to be invulnerable."

I couldn't think of one. Who *wouldn't* want to be invulnerable?

She paused. "And I don't think you understand how it works. In order to be safe from death, you have to experience death first."

"What?" Now she had shaken me. Avoiding death was the whole reason I was doing this.

I had found her ad in the back pages of a psychic cult magazine. But she had not advertised herself as a psychic. "Freedom from Death" was all the ad had said. And that's what interested me.

It had started a long time ago with a half-remembered folktale about a monster who hides his soul in some completely inaccessible place—inside a marble egg, locked in a secret cave high in the mountains, someplace like that. He could come to no harm, he could live forever, no matter what his enemies tried to do to his body, until someone found where his soul was hidden and destroyed it. This being a folktale, the human hero *did* find the monster's soul eventually, and the monster got killed. I didn't like that ending. I would have preferred the monster to go on living forever. In any case, the story stuck with me through the years.

And then, two weeks ago, my best friend Roger died in a plane crash. Not everyone on the plane died; Roger was one of the unlucky ones. It was the worst thing that had happened to me. Somebody my own age, sixteen, my best friend, dying. It was unthinkable. At first I couldn't accept it; I tried to convince myself that it was a dream, that it couldn't really have happened. Mom and Dad tried to be kind but they also had to be firm. The funeral finally convinced me—Roger's mother and father and his sister and brother all crying, and the coffin, and no Roger. I didn't cry. I also didn't say anything to anyone. People understood, and left me alone.

But now I knew that if Roger could die, I could die, too. And I kept thinking about that folktale.

I was frantic. I counted my money, and started with psychics. I didn't call the ones on TV—they seemed so flamboyant and phony and commercial. I looked for little ads in the phone book and various newspapers. A lot of them thought I was too young and refused to talk to me. The ones who did listen didn't pay attention to what I wanted—they thought I wanted to talk to Roger, or else that I had a crush on some girl and wouldn't admit it. I knew I couldn't talk to Roger; he was dead. None of them were any help at all.

Until I found this one, Cheri Buttercup, in a high-rise apartment in Queens. I'd had a lot of trouble getting there. She told me on the phone which train to take on the Long Island Rail Road, and which stop to get off at, and said to get a cab behind the station there. But there were no cabs, and it was raining, and the neighborhood looked seedy and dangerous. No one wanted to help me; people didn't talk to each other on the street around here. I took a bus, and then I realized it was going the wrong way, so I had to get off and cross the busy street.

And when I was halfway across the street I heard the squealing of tires and turned and saw a car running a red light and heading directly at me; the driver was watching for other cars and didn't see me. I jumped back just in time and actually felt the sideview mirror brush against me. My heart was pounding as I waited for a bus going the other way, drenched, suspicious of all the people around me. I had to get this done before something else happened!

When the bus finally came I asked the driver to tell me when we got to her apartment complex, but he didn't tell me, and when I finally asked him if we had gone past it, we had, and I had to walk a long way uphill in the rain. Cheri Buttercup seemed nervous that I arrived so late—she didn't understand that rain made all public transportation slower.

So it wasn't a good start. And her apartment really put me off. No beaded curtains or crystal balls here! It was a modern high-rise, and the room was full of puffy leather furniture, and had a pink shag carpet, and statues of ballerinas, and knitted tissue box covers. There were mirrors everywhere—the coffee table had a mirrored surface; there were little mirrors in the cabinets behind the ballerina statues and other knickknacks. I kept catching glimpses of my mouth, or my hand—or her pale eyes, watching me. The place reeked of cigarette smoke. And she looked like somebody who went to lunch a lot with other ladies her own age, in her hairdo and makeup.

But she had been the only one I called who understood what I meant about hiding my soul and being safe from death, and at fifty dollars she was amazingly cheap, compared to the other ones I talked to, who all would have charged two hundred dollars just for me to come to see them.

But now she was telling me I had to die first. Forget it. I started to get up.

But where else was I going to go? There didn't seem to be any other possibilities. I sank back into the puffy leather couch. "What are you talking about? *How* do I die first? And if I really die, how can I come back?"

She watched me, unsmiling. "You can't expect to get something this big without a sacrifice. Money isn't the issue," she said, and lifted her hand. She wore a lot of rings with big showy jewels on them. "Death is part of the ritual. It has to be that way. I can't hide your soul unless I take it out first. It doesn't last long. And you will come back, I promise you, and be safe forever. I've done it . . . a lot of times. One hundred percent success rate."

Could I believe her? Did I dare? But why should she want to kill me? It was a huge risk for her to take, if I really died and didn't come back. And what would she get out of it? A credit card for a day and a few more dollars. It didn't look like she needed that.

I leaned forward. "Where would you hide my soul?" I asked her. I had to know. I had to be in some kind of control.

"Oh." She seemed surprised. "But you have to understand. I can't tell you *where* I'm going to hide your soul. If you knew, you might end up telling somebody else, or you might try to go there yourself and get it back." She half smiled. "Uh-uh, honey. Everything has to be done through me."

Did I really want *her* to be the only one who knew? "But I won't try to get it back, and I won't tell anybody," I insisted. "I swear it. I want to know where it is. After all, it's my own soul."

"Not after you pay me," she said, looking at her bright pink fingernails—her toenails, in high-heeled slippers, were the same horrible color.

"Now wait a minute," I said. "I'm the one who's paying. I want to know exactly what—"

She held up her bejeweled hand to shush me. "Don't get all bent out of shape," she said. "It's not like you're selling your soul to the Devil or anything like that. I've just learned from experience that it's safer if the client doesn't know where it is. That's the deal. Take it or leave it."

I didn't like ultimatums. Nobody gave me ultimatums. I could feel the hard knot of anger in my stomach. I wanted to tell this horrible woman to take her ultimatum and shove it, and then walk out of there for good.

But Roger had just died, and a car had almost killed me on the way here. And she was the only person I had found who said she would do this for me—despite what I had to go through to get it.

I sighed, forcing myself to be calm and not tell her off. I fought to keep my voice under control. "But what happens, exactly?" I said. And I couldn't resist adding, "I don't like the sound of it—at all."

Now she smiled. "Nobody does, honey. But you can't cheat death. You have to pay your dues."

"You didn't answer my question about how it happens," I reminded her, my voice rising.

"Aw right awready," she said. "I just sprinkle a little powder on you. It puts you out. It doesn't last for long. That's when I take out your soul and hide it. And then I give you a paste to eat, and you come out of it. And it's all over. You're safe forever."

I was still skeptical—and scared. "But what do *you* get out of it?" I wanted to know. Fifty dollars obviously didn't mean a lot to her.

"You pay me," she said. "I'm a practitioner of a rare art, which gives me pleasure. And I'm doing a good deed—protecting you forever."

Did I dare to believe her? The alternative was to go out into this dangerous world *without* protection. I thought about Roger's funeral. They had had a closed casket. They'd had to.

I pushed all my doubts aside. "Okay, okay. Let's just do it and get it over with," I said. I sat back carefully on the couch.

She looked at me with her cold blue eyes. "I see you're used to getting your own way," she said. "You're going to have to learn to make compromises—especially after this." She got up. "You just wait right there. I'll be back in a sec." She left the room.

I sat there looking at all the knickknacks, and my fractured reflections in the dimness. I looked younger and more frightened than I liked.

Cheri Buttercup returned in a minute. She carried a glass jar with a bright red cloth draped over it. "You said you're doing this because your friend died in a plane crash two weeks ago, and that scared you," she said. "What was his name?"

Why did she want to know Roger's name? But I couldn't see any reason not to tell her. "Roger Kelly," I said.

"Lie down," she said. "Unbutton the top of your shirt."

Now I was really scared. "I'm . . . I'm not really going to die, am I?" I asked her.

She sighed. "Do you want to do this or not? Make up your mind."

She was treating me like a child. I wasn't a child and I wasn't going to show her how scared I was. I lay down on the soft leather couch and unbuttoned my shirt.

She didn't just sprinkle the powder on me, she rubbed it in, hard. I could feel her fingernails scratching my skin. I hated it. But I couldn't deny that what she said made sense. Being safe from death was big. You would have to go through something *else* big to achieve it.

After five minutes of rubbing and scratching she left the room again, carrying her jar. She wasn't even waiting around to see what was happening to me?

I begin to feel cold. At first I think it's just because I'm afraid. Then I know it's a lot more than that. My temperature is dropping. I try to take a deep breath but it won't come. My breathing grows shallower and shallower, until I'm hardly breathing at all. I feel like choking, but I can't choke.

And then another sensation begins in my fingers and toes, and runs up my arms and legs. It feels like insects are crawling under my skin. It's unbearable. I want to scratch at it, to slap it away. But I can't move.

Cold as I am, a terrible fear burns through me. I'm paralyzed. It's like that half dream state when no matter how hard you try, you can't bend a muscle. But this isn't a dream. I'm cold, I'm hardly breathing, and I'm stiff as a stone. And bugs are running under my skin. It's the worst thing I've ever felt in my life. And what if she's wrong, and I stay like this forever? I'm panicking. But I still can't move or speak.

And then, slowly, I rise into the air, floating above the couch. It isn't my physical self that's floating—I know my body is lying below me, stiff and cold on the cold leather. The part of me that's floating is separate from my body. But at the same time I can still feel the physical sensations running through me.

Cheri Buttercup comes back into the room. She leans over my body. She takes hold of my wrist and feels my pulse. Then she bends her ear to my chest. She nods, pursing her lips, as if satisfied. Then she sits down in her chair and picks up the phone, mumbling into it for a few minutes. It sounds like she's giving instructions, but she's careful to make sure I can't hear what she's saying.

She hangs up and goes out of the room and comes back again with a pack of cigarettes and a little nail-care kit. She lights a cigarette and lets it hang from her lips as she files and buffs her nails—they must have broken a little from the way she was scratching the powder into me. When she finishes with her nails she gets a compact from the table next to the chair and looks in the mirror while she puts on lipstick and then presses her lips together. She doesn't seem the least bit concerned about what's happening to me. I still feel the insects crawling under my skin.

Is this what death is like? I want to shout at her but I can't move or talk. Even though I can feel my body, I'm not part of it anymore.

Finally she checks her watch. Then she stands over me and slips a gold chain off her neck and holds it up. It has some sparkly jewel on the end of it that casts a dancing, flickering light around the room. It zips across the ceiling and away.

And then the part of me that was floating is gone. All that's left is my body, still paralyzed on the couch.

Cheri Buttercup leaves the room and comes back with a ceramic vessel, rounded, like a mortar. She leans over me and with a very small white rubber spatula rubs something from the mortar around on my lips, forcing it into my mouth, which doesn't want to open, but somehow does. She rubs it onto my tongue. She leaves the room again.

I swallow. Something gooey, sweet and bitter at the same time, goes down my throat. Almost immediately I begin to feel warm. My breathing increases. The insects stop crawling under my skin.

I sat up. Cheri Buttercup was watching me from her chair. I quickly buttoned my shirt. Why was it unbuttoned? I could see there was something on my chest, but I didn't want to study it now, I just wanted to get out of here.

"Fifty dollars, please," Cheri Buttercup said. "I have another client coming soon."

"Did it work?"

"Can't you feel it?" she said, smiling her hard smile.

It's not easy to explain how I felt. It was something like being hungry, as though I hadn't eaten anything all day and my stomach was empty. But I didn't want to eat; I didn't want to fill the emptiness. I felt strangely light-headed—and lighthearted, too. I wouldn't call it happiness. The way I felt was too devoid of emotion to be exactly happy. But a weight had been taken away—the weight that had been there since Roger had died.

Something really had changed deeply. I wanted to get out of this stuffy, smoky place and walk in the rain.

I stood up and pulled out my wallet and handed her fifty dollars. As she took the money I noticed that her pink fingernails were very long, and perfectly curved.

She stood up to usher me toward the door. I looked around the room again. I wondered how she could afford all this expensive, useless junk if she charged only fifty dollars.

"You're sure?" I asked her. "You really did it? My soul is safe now?"

"Believe me, kiddo, it's safe. And so are you. Nothing and nobody can hurt you now."

"How do I know? How can you prove it?" I demanded. And I was thinking, *You can't hurt somebody who's dead.*

She opened the door. "You'll find out soon enough."

I believed her. I felt like a different person now, colder, harder. "Well, 'bye," I said. "Thanks."

"See you later," she said, and carefully shut and locked the door.

two

It had stopped raining now, and I hadn't felt this empty of bad feelings since Roger had died. I decided to skip the bus and walk to the train station. I was so full of energy that I was practically jogging.

On the subway platform at Penn Station, Thirty-fourth Street, I wondered what chain of events I would set off if I threw myself in front of the oncoming train. It was an interesting thought, but I wasn't ready to test Cheri Buttercup's magic in that dangerous a way—yet.

We lived in a large brick building on a quiet, tree-lined street in Greenwich Village, the arty part of Manhattan, where they didn't have skyscrapers, and everything was pretty expensive. Our apartment was the top two floors of the building, the penthouse duplex.

The top floor was the living area, a big open loft with a wall of windows that gave a great view of the city. The kitchen had granite counters and a chrome refrigerator and a big gas stove. Most New York apartments have one small bedroom and a closet-sized kitchen and a view of a wall. I had always taken living in this place for granted until the last few years. I went to a private school, and most of the kids there were pretty well-off, but not a whole lot of their apartments were as big and nice as ours. The first time I brought a kid over he'd usually be pretty impressed. I liked that.

The lower floor was where the bedrooms were. As I let myself in I could hear the TV from upstairs, and smelled cooking food coming down from the kitchen. I hung my jacket in the closet and went into my bedroom and closed the door.

Standing in front of the mirror I unbuttoned my shirt. There were scratches on my chest—black, crusted scratches that looked really ugly. How had they gotten there? It could only have been part of the ritual Cheri Buttercup had performed on me that I couldn't remember. I hoped they would go away soon. I swam several times a week and the other people in the pool would wonder about them, maybe even not want me in the water. I did my best to cover them with bandages but it still looked weird. Why had she done this to me?

I had to go upstairs and deal with Mom and Dad, and figure out where to tell them I had been. Not that it mattered much. They mostly let me do as I pleased, and believed a sixteen-year-old was mature enough to be out late on a Saturday afternoon without much explanation. I wondered if Cheri Buttercup had been right when she said I was used to having my own way. I had never thought about it. But now that I did, I realized that there wasn't much of anything I wanted that I didn't end up getting. Did that mean I was spoiled?

I didn't feel like thinking about that now. I was too eager to know if the ritual had worked. Anyway, what difference did it make if I was spoiled or not? If I was invulnerable I could do anything, have anything. And I'd always get away with it.

I went up the stairs two at a time. Mom was cooking in the open kitchen; Dad was on one of the two big off-white couches watching TV. I plopped myself down on the other couch. On TV was a Discovery Channel show about sharks. I thought about swimming in shark infested waters; that would be amazing.

"So where were you out on this lousy Saturday afternoon?" Dad asked me.

"Just around," I said.

He looked over toward the kitchen and I knew they were exchanging a glance. They were relaxed with me, but maybe that wasn't a good enough answer, even for them.

"At a friend's house," I said. "Er . . . Toby Adams," I added. He was a junior who went out with the hottest girl at our school. He wasn't my friend.

Dad smiled and leaned back on the couch. "Well, good to see you getting out and about again, Ken. You've been pretty solitary for the last few weeks." He didn't mention the reason why, not wanting to bring up Roger's death. As if I'd forgotten.

I looked at the sharks and thought about what might happen if one of them tried to bite my leg off. How could I find out if I were truly invulnerable without actually hurting myself? I was imagining ways when Mom called us in to dinner.

She took a hot dish out of the oven with two thick pot holders and set it down on a metal trivet on the table. She sat down.

I wasn't particularly hungry, but I didn't feel like waiting. I reached over and without thinking I slowly and carefully pulled the dish of bubbling baked cannelloni toward me.

"Ken! Be careful!" Mom cried out. "I just took that out of a four-hundred-and-fifty-degree oven!"

I held it for another second, confused, and then let go. I hadn't felt a thing. I shook my hand, pretending it had been burned.

"Oh, let me see what you did to yourself," Mom said, and before I could stop her she grabbed my hand and examined it. She looked back at my face, puzzled. "No burn, no redness, no blister, nothing. And I could feel the heat of that dish through those heavy pot holders half a minute ago."

I stared at my hand and then at my mother's confused expression. I wanted to grab the dish again to be sure it couldn't burn me, but my parents would think I was nuts.

"I, er, guess I didn't touch it long enough," I said. "I better put my hand in cold water, though. It really hurts."

They were whispering as I stood at the sink, running cold water over my hand. They must have noticed that I hadn't instantly let go of the burning hot dish. I was going to have to test myself in private.

After supper, while Mom and Dad started to clean up, I went back down to my room and closed the door. I kept a pair of nail scissors on my desk because I used the computer a lot and liked to keep my fingernails really short because it was easier to type that way. I picked up the scissors and hesitated. I was pretty sure the ritual had worked because I hadn't burned my hand on the dish of cannelloni. But I still wasn't one hundred percent sure—and I had to be, before I did anything really dangerous.

I stared at the scissors. If they *did* cut me, where would be the least noticeable place?

My chest, of course. There were already those black scratches there. One little cut wouldn't make any difference alongside them.

I unbuttoned my shirt and held the scissors open. I gritted my teeth and pushed the scissors against my right pectoral muscle. Nothing happened. I didn't even feel it. I jabbed them into the muscle. Nothing. I scraped them hard, really hard, across the skin. Not a scratch.

The scissors weren't piercing my skin. But I still had to be totally sure. And I was more daring now. I held the scissors in the normal way and tried as hard as I could to cut off my right nipple.

It was like trying to cut a stone.

Cheri Buttercup had done it all right. Now I knew I could do anything and I wouldn't get hurt.

But I didn't feel like jumping up and down and whooping with glee, as I would have expected. I felt only a kind of cold satisfaction.

I gave Kaitlin a big smile when I saw her in home room on Monday. "You have a good weekend?" I asked her.

She smiled back carefully. She wasn't the brightest, but she sure was beautiful, with long blonde hair and a great body. And she had a super jealous boyfriend, Toby Adams, a two-hundred-pound football player. The kind of guy who would stuff you upside down inside a locker for looking at his girlfriend twice. I had the perfect plan for showing the whole school that I could beat him.

"Toby and I went to see a show on Broadway," she said. "It was really cool."

"What show?"

She frowned prettily. "Er, I forget the name. But it was really cool. Lots of guys fighting, and—"

The final bell rang.

"Want to go to a show with me next weekend?" I asked Kaitlin, before we sat down.

She looked confused, but she didn't instantly say no, which surprised me.

"So next Friday, is it a date?" I asked Kaitlin after class, making sure the kids around us could hear.

"But . . . Toby wouldn't like it," she said.

"He doesn't own you, right?"

"No," she said. "But . . . he's bigger than you, and he likes to fight. If I went out with you, you might get hurt."

"Don't worry about it," I said coolly.

She smiled. She looked like she was about to laugh it off. Then she paused and said, "Hey, why not? Friday would be cool." She walked off to her next class.

I had a date with Kaitlin Marsh. I couldn't believe it. Did she actually like me? And now I had a fight, too. Toby Adams was going to try to kick my ass. I couldn't wait.

Toby Adams sauntered over to me in the courtyard after lunch. He was big, half a head taller than me and about fifty pounds heavier—he'd been on the varsity football team since he was a freshman.

"I hear you had a conversation with Kaitlin this morning, creep," he said. "Want to take back what you said now?"

"So I asked her out," I said. "What's the big deal?"

A lot of kids were watching now, but nobody was getting very close.

"Do you own her?" I asked.

"Hey, Pritchard, are you crazy!" Andy called out. He was a friend of Roger's and mine. We'd sat together at the funeral but kind of avoided each other since. "Back off. He'll kill you!"

"I can tell her I don't want her to talk to a creep like you," Toby Adams said. "And I'll kick the crap out of you if you don't beg me not to in front of everybody."

"You can't tell me I can't ask her out," I said. I couldn't wait for his first punch.

"I'm giving you one more chance." He moved closer.

"Threaten me all you want," I told him. "I'm going out with Kaitlin on Friday."

He hit my shoulder with one hand to push me back. It felt like being stroked with a feather. I didn't move an inch.

And he pulled back his hand as if he'd tried to push a brick wall. Suddenly his face was red. He made a fist, and then came the punch to the chin.

Another feather.

But to him it must have felt like he'd punched a cement block. He grabbed his fist with his other hand, wringing it, grimacing, hunched over in pain. In that position it was easy for me to put one foot behind him and push him to the pavement.

He jumped up and went for my throat with both hands. I stood there as he squeezed and shook my neck, and felt nothing. After a minute he backed away, panting, his shoulders sagging. I just stood there. I didn't need to say anything now.

Then he stood up straight and looked at me hard. "I don't know what got into you today, but I'll tell you one thing," he said, breathing hard. "You won't be going out with her on Friday because you're gonna be in the hospital then." He turned and stalked away, not meeting anyone's eye.

Oddly, I didn't feel elated by my victory; I just felt sort of hollow. And none of the other kids cheered or anything. They didn't want to risk it with Adams. But he had never been humiliated like this before. And I was smarter than him and knew that he and some of his football-playing friends were going to attack me when they thought I wasn't expecting it. Then they'd be even more surprised.

"How'd you *do* that?" Andy wanted to know, as we went back inside the building. Adams was gone and kids were clustered around me. "It was like . . . something in the movies."

"Oh." I hadn't thought about how I was going to explain it; I just thought it would make me the hero of the school. "Martial arts," I said, thinking fast. "I've been taking lessons, and practicing every day. You don't have to be big. It's just discipline."

"Yeah?" Andy said skeptically. He and the other kids looked puzzled. I didn't know if they were buying it or not.

Kaitlin found me at my locker in the crowded hallway after school. "I heard about what happened with you and Toby at lunch," she said hurriedly. "I don't know how you did it, but now he's really mad. He's a jerk when he's mad. You're going to get hurt really bad. It's not worth it, Ken. We can't go out."

"Everything's going to be okay. You'll see," I assured her, smiling. "See you on Friday."

She looked at me strangely but didn't disagree. Then she hurried away, obviously not wanting Toby to catch us together.

I got home without incident. It was what I expected. They wouldn't strike today; it was too soon. They wanted to wait until they thought I'd forgotten. Did they think I was stupid?

At home I surfed the Internet. It was starting to get cold again, more normal for this time of year, and I'd decided a warm place would be great for spring break. My parents always let me pick the place. I had never gone scuba diving before. When I did a search for good places to dive, the first thing that appeared on my screen was a small island in the Caribbean called St. Calao that had spectacular reefs—there were underwater pictures—and you could get certified to scuba dive right there.

Snorkeling was okay, but with real scuba gear you could be way down there, right among the sharks and barracuda and stinging jellyfish and prickly sea anemones.

There was also a little warning notice to click, not part of the St. Calao advertising. It said there had been a shark attack there a month ago, and to be careful. I felt my pulse pick up. This was the place.

I told Mom and Dad about it at dinner—except for the part about the shark attack.

"I think I've heard about it," Dad said. "I can arrange the whole thing on the Web. What week are you off?"

"First week in March. But why don't you let me arrange it, Dad? I'd like to. I'm good with computers and you're so busy." I didn't want him to see the warning.

I could see he was excited—he was so glad I was interested in life again. "There's still time, if it's not all booked already. That'll be the problem. But you can handle it. You're better online than I am. Tomorrow I'll arrange to get the time off from work. No problem at the firm—I'm the boss." He chuckled. People said I took after him.

Kaitlin was distant in school the next couple of days. I actually felt kind of hurt, but then it struck me that she was probably just trying to protect me. Part of her had to like it that Adams and I were fighting over her—what girl wouldn't? But she was also clearly worried about me, and trying to stay away from me in order to protect me. That was sweet of her. She would find out soon enough that it wasn't necessary.

But the other kids kept their distance, too. I didn't understand it. Before Roger died, he and Andy and I used to hang out after school pretty often. I hadn't felt like doing that after Roger died. And I knew that I'd avoided Andy more than he'd avoided me. Now, when *I* suggested we go get something to eat, he said he was busy.

It had to be because I was Adams's enemy now. He'd get friendly again when I got Adams out of the picture. But I still had that hollow feeling. Okay, I was invulnerable. But that didn't make me stop missing Roger, and our long conversations about everything. He had been the only person I felt really understood me. I wondered what he'd think of what I was doing now. Somehow, hard as I tried, I couldn't imagine him saying "This is awesome, Ken," the way he had when we'd hacked into a pay-to-play game site.

I also had the funny feeling that everybody had liked me better before Roger died.

I was late getting out of school on Wednesday, because of the computer club. It was dark when I left the school building. There weren't many kids around now so it was easy to see when a group of five big guys stepped out from behind a corner of the building where they had been waiting for me.

If I'd been scared I could have hurried straight out to the busy, well-lit sidewalk. But I wasn't scared. I was full of excited tension. So I took the way through the deserted, dark little park next to the school. They must have thought I didn't know they were behind me.

And then, suddenly, in the middle of the park where it was darkest, and where the pathways met in a round, paved area, they appeared in front of me. It was like a football play. The five of them stood there, blocking my way, Adams in the middle.

I pretended to act surprised. "Hey, where'd you guys come from?"

"I'm giving you one more chance, Pritchard," Adams said. "'Cause I've heard you've gone crazy over your dead friend. You gonna lay off Kaitlin now?"

The four other guys were even bigger than he was. This was going to be a real test. For a moment I wondered if it would work. What if they had knives? Well, so what if they did?

I shrugged. Screw him for bringing up Roger. "Kaitlin and I have a date on Friday night, dude," I said. "I thought I told you that already."

Adams shook his head in disbelief. "So you're really asking for it, huh?"

"I just said I was going on a date. And now I gotta get home."

"Sure . . . by ambulance," Adams said. And then they moved.

I started to run, so they'd think I was scared. I was learning—a little. That gave them the chance to tackle me. I relaxed and let myself go down. My books scattered, and it was interesting *not* to feel the skin of my face scrape against the pavement. They rolled me over on my back and started kicking, hard. They were concentrating on my gut and my head. The rotten jerks! They could have hurt my kidneys, they could have caused internal bleeding in my brain. I was glad to be doing this to Adams. I hadn't realized he was this bad. He deserved all the humiliation he was going to get.

Two of them were pinning me down, one with my hands and one with my feet, and the other three, especially Adams, were doing the kicking. I didn't feel a thing, and the ones who were trying to kick me were already grunting in pain—my body was hurting them even through their shoes. After about fifteen seconds I pulled away from the guys holding me down, kicked out hard at Adams's gut, and jumped to my feet. Then they held my arms behind me, standing up, so Adams could punch me all over. After a few seconds he backed away, like before, holding his fist in pain. Other guys tried to hit me, and the same thing happened. The guys holding me couldn't understand it, and they tried punching me, too. It was only a couple of minutes before they were all backing away, totally bewildered. I calmly picked up my books while they stood there. They weren't saying anything, to me or to each other. It was like they were in shock.

"See you guys later," I said, and turned my back on them and started walking away.

Adams ran after me and pulled me around to face him, panting. He didn't try to punch me now; he didn't want to hurt his hands any more. "What . . . what is it with you?" he said, shaking his head, looking scared.

The same problem again: There was no way to explain. Being invulnerable wasn't as easy as I had imagined. I fell back on the same lame excuse. "Martial arts. I've been taking classes. There's two parts to it—hurting the attackers, and just not letting them hurt you. Lucky for you I've only been doing the second part. The first part comes next if you ever try anything like this again."

The other guys were clustered around me, too, looking as puzzled and scared as Adams. "Martial arts?" he said. "But you weren't doing any kick-boxing or anything."

"I told you, I was just protecting myself, not trying to hurt you guys—this time. This training is something new. It's sort of like yoga. I found out about it on the Web."

He glared at me, still not convinced. "What's it called? What's the Web site?" he wanted to know.

"Oh, come on," I said. "You think I'm going to tell you that?"

I could feel he wanted to punch me again, but of course he didn't. He knew he couldn't get at me, no matter what I did. "All right, all right, go out with her on Friday," Adams said, not meeting my eye. "But do me a favor." He turned and looked at the other guys, then back toward me, still not looking directly at me. "-Don't . . . Don't tell anybody about this. Okay?" His voice was really low now; he hated demeaning himself by asking me to do this. "The other day was bad enough, in front of everybody. I'm letting you go out with her. You owe me enough not to spread this around the whole school."

I wanted to laugh. *He* was letting *me* go out with her? Well, let him try to boost his shattered ego. I could be big and not tell anybody about their pathetic attempt to get me. I shrugged. "Sure. No reason for anybody to know. I can be big about it." I lifted my hand. "See you guys later." I turned and walked casually away from them, whistling.

But the weird thing was, I didn't feel full of jubilation now, not even the cold jubilation I had felt when I had tried and failed to cut off my nipple. There was something different about this, something that made me feel uncomfortable in a way I didn't understand.

I thought about Roger. He had always told me I took everything too seriously. But we had laughed together, too. There hadn't exactly been anything to laugh at since he died. Until now. But I still didn't feel like laughing at Toby.

"You beat them, you jerk," I told myself, aloud.
But it didn't make me feel any better, either.

three

I'm lying in some kind of box, and I'm paralyzed—
I can't move an arm, a leg, a finger. I have no voice, because my breathing is so shallow it's like I'm hardly aware of breathing at all. I feel very cold. My temperature is so far below normal that if I weren't paralyzed I'd be shivering uncontrollably. I have the disgusting sensation that bugs are crawling under my skin, but I can't move to scratch.

And then everything goes black when they fit a cover onto the box. Now I understand: They think I'm dead, and they're burying me in a coffin. I try to scream, to bang on the lid of the coffin as I hear the nails being pounded in, the coffin shaking with each slam of the hammer. But I can't move; I can't make a sound. They really think I'm dead! And now they're lowering the coffin into the ground. In a moment something heavy and porous falls down on top of the coffin. Earth. They're burying me alive. I'm doing everything in my power to scream and bang but I can't move and I can't make a sound.

But when I woke up I *was* screaming, "Dunwich! Dunwich!" even though I had no idea what it meant. And in a moment Mom and Dad rushed into my room in bathrobes. "Just a bad dream. Not a big deal," I kept telling them, until they finally went away.

But I had never had a dream so realistic and so horrifying in my life—not until I had become invulnerable.

Adams must have said something to Kaitlin because the next day she was friendlier than she had ever been. Maybe she hadn't really liked Adams—who could?—and had just dated him because he was older and on the football team. I swam a lot and went out for track. I was smarter and more interesting than Adams was. Maybe I actually had a shot with her.

We went to see a show called *Blue Man Group*. Mom charged the tickets for me, she was so happy I was going out. *Blue Man Group* had been playing for years, but neither Kaitlin nor I had seen it. Neither of us was big on theater, I guess. But I was determined to take her to a show because that's what Adams had done.

We had dinner first, at a steak house near the theater that Dad had told me about. I wasn't really hungry but I got a steak. Kaitlin had broiled fish, which seemed like a waste to me, but she was a girl and I knew girls were always thinking about not being fat. "Did you go to as nice a place with Toby?" I asked her.

She seemed a little surprised. "Different," she said. "A burger place. Not this expensive."

Just what I wanted to hear. We didn't talk much about the other kids at school, for some reason. We discussed the teachers, which wasn't all that exciting. I tried to talk about computers, but all Kaitlin knew about them was how to do e-mail and instant messaging. She said IM was the best way to gossip, since nobody else could know what you were saying about them.

Finally she asked me, "What happened with Toby, anyway? Why did he tell me he *wanted* me to go out with you?"

I remembered how weird I had felt after he and his friends had tried to attack me. I really didn't want to tell her anything about that, and not just because I had promised Toby I wouldn't mention it to anybody. If I told her, how would I explain why they hadn't beaten me into a bloodfest? I shrugged. "I don't know much about Toby," I said. "Maybe he just caught on that, like, you aren't his property, so no reason not to go out with me."

"Funny," she said. "That's not like him."

I was glad that our food came then and we could busy ourselves with eating, and talking about the food.

When we got to the theater and picked up the tickets it turned out we had seats in the center of the orchestra. "Did you have seats this good when you went out with Toby?" I couldn't keep myself from asking her, after we sat down.

She looked at me, not smiling. "No, they weren't as good," she said, and suddenly I wished I hadn't asked her about the theater *and* the restaurant. But right away she perked up again. "This is exciting. Look how crowded it is!"

The show was these three guys who were all blue—not just their clothes, all their skin and faces and heads were blue too, and they were all bald. They beat these things that looked like drums, except that when they hit them something like paint, all different colors, sprayed out of them, like fire in the stage lights, getting all over everything on the stage. They also did things with these strange tubes. It was pretty weird and meaningless, but the audience loved it, laughing and screaming, and people from the audience went up on stage and got splashed, too. I tried to pretend I really liked it, but I just kept thinking about that terrible dream of being buried alive. Kaitlin was laughing and *oohing* and *aahing,* but I had the feeling she was pretending, too.

I would have liked to take her for a walk in the middle of Central Park late at night, to show her how brave I was, but it was the opposite direction from the Village, where we both lived, and we both had curfews, so we didn't have a lot of time. At the doorway to her building I put my arm around her and then hesitated. Now I was nervous.

Finally she said, "Oh, go ahead and kiss me, Ken," and I did. She put her arms around me, too, and it felt okay, but not as great as I expected. It lasted only a minute or two, and she went inside, thanking me for a great time.

As I walked home I wondered if I was a decent kisser. What Cheri Buttercup had done wasn't going to help me with that.

And why hadn't I enjoyed kissing Kaitlin, a complete hottie? It was mystifying: She was so much better looking than anyone I had ever gone out with. What was the matter with me? Could *this* have something to do with being invulnerable, too?

Kaitlin sent me an e-mail the next day:

Hey Ken,

Thanks for a great time. I'd like to see you again. But just wanted to tell you, I'm going out with Toby tonight. That doesn't mean I don't like you.

Bye,
Kaitlin

My first reaction was anger. He had a lot of nerve, after I showed him who was boss. I started writing back to her that her going out with Toby *was* a problem.

Then I thought about what Roger would have told me to do, and luckily deleted that e-mail. If I told her not to go out with him, it would be like I was asking her to go out just with me, and I hadn't really meant to get involved with her in the first place. She was beautiful but I had to admit that our date had been seriously dull. And maybe she actually liked the thug.

I wrote back that I had a great time, too, and would talk to her at school. I'd worry about what to say to her later.

Meanwhile, I had worked things out and gotten the plane tickets and the resort reservations for St. Calao. It was remarkably easy to get inexpensive rooms right on the water, including scuba instruction and certification—probably because most tourists were afraid to go there now because of that shark warning. Sixteen was the cutoff age for scuba certification, which was really lucky, but you had to take a swimming test before they would even consider it. That wasn't a problem; our school didn't have a pool, but Dad had pulled strings so that I could use the NYU pool, and I swam there at least three times a week to get in shape. I knew I would pass their stupid test, even though I hadn't gone swimming since Cheri Buttercup had scratched me. The scratch marks were getting smaller now, but slowly. I worried they might not be gone by the time we went to St. Calao. Then what would I do? Maybe the other people wouldn't care, but I couldn't let Mom and Dad see them.

I told them it had been hard to find good reservations on St. Calao, but I had persisted and been persuasive, and finally got them. They were impressed.

On Sunday afternoon Andy finally agreed to go with me to this Internet café where we used to hang out and drink coffee. But it wasn't the same. One problem was that this was the first time we had come here since Roger had died, and we were both really aware of that, though we didn't say a word about him.

The other problem was the whole situation between Adams and

Kaitlin and me. Andy still didn't understand how I had defended myself, and gotten a date with her. I tried to distract him by telling him about the show, and how I had kissed her for more than ten minutes. He kept bringing the conversation back to this martial arts stuff I was supposedly studying. I had no excuse not to tell him about it—the way I had an excuse not to tell Adams. Naturally Andy wanted to know how to defend himself the way I had, what the training was called, where the Web site was, and especially where the martial arts studio was. He wanted me to bring him with me the next time I went! How could I deal with this? I had never thought about this problem when I started the whole thing with Cheri Buttercup. Nothing was turning out as good as I had expected.

Should I tell him the truth? If I did, he'd think I was crazy. And if he didn't think I was crazy, he'd go see Cheri Buttercup, too. And there was no way he wouldn't tell other kids about it. And then everybody in the school would do it. Cheri Buttercup would probably love all that business, but I didn't care about her business. If everybody started doing it, then I'd have no advantage at all. Telling him the truth was out.

Finally I said, "Well, see, Andy, it's this kind of exclusive thing. My father got me into it, through his connections." He knew my father was a high-powered lawyer. "Like, the people who teach it don't want a lot of people to know how to do it. They have money, they're not into new clients. If everybody could do it, then it wouldn't be worth much anymore. Think about it. See what I mean? And so you have to sign this agreement not to tell anybody. I know that sounds jerky, but there's not much I can do. I had to promise."

He gave me a funny look. "So then why are they teaching it to *anybody,* if they don't need the money, and they don't want people to know about it? Yeah, I'm thinking about it. And it doesn't make sense."

He didn't believe me. It was like he was accusing me of lying to him. I didn't like that. I stood up. "Sorry, Andy. That's just the way it is," I said, my voice rising. "There's nothing else I can tell you." I turned and walked out of the place.

I was angry. But it didn't feel good to be angry. It felt lousy. All the other guys I knew would want to know the same thing. And they wouldn't believe what I told them and that would make me angry again. Did that mean I wasn't going to have friends anymore?

Now I understood why Cheri Buttercup had asked me to think about all the consequences. I began to wonder what she meant about how hard it was to get your soul back again. Hiding it in the first place had been bad enough, lying there unconscious in her apartment for an hour, while she had scratched me. Now I was mad at that old bag, too. I wanted to go back there and complain, but it was too much trouble to go to Queens.

At homeroom on Monday Kaitlin came right up to me, smiling. I tried to be pleasant, even though I just wanted to get away from her. "Hey, there's this 3-D horror picture at the Imax theater," she said. "Maybe we could go on Friday."

"Uh, sorry," I told her. "I have this commitment with my parents—for the whole weekend."

She looked disappointed. And after class I got out of there fast without talking to her. I had no interest in her anymore—I had only gone out with her in order to beat Adams. It had been a bad mistake, and now all my former friends were mad at me, too. I avoided her, and before long she knew it and was avoiding me. I just wanted things between her and Adams to go back to normal.

All I cared about now was going to St. Calao.

four

St. Calao is a small island. It's not a place where any big cruise ships go, or where people explore quaint villages and stay at big fancy resorts and spend a lot of time eating gourmet food and lying around on the beach. It's mainly for serious scuba diving enthusiasts, because of the spectacular reef—and serious marine scientists, because of the sharks, which Mom and Dad didn't know about. So none of the big airlines go there.

There was a big storm on the Friday afternoon we left for St. Calao. The flight to Miami wasn't so bad—we were on a big jet and it wasn't very bumpy. But there was more wind and rain in Miami than in New York, and we had to take a small plane on an airline we had never heard of before—it was the only way to get to St.

Calao. At least it was a little jet, not a prop. Mom probably wouldn't have gotten *on* the plane if it had been a prop.

The plane was so small that one side had only one seat, and the other side had two. Of course I sat in the single seat and Mom and Dad sat together across the narrow aisle from me. The fact that we weren't all sitting together made it more possible that if something did happen, Mom and Dad could get hurt and I'd be okay. I didn't like that.

And as the plane taxied down the runway, water streaming down the dark windows, I thought about all the things that had happened since Cheri Buttercup had worked her magic on me. Yeah, some of it had been good, in a way. But most of it had backfired in ways I hadn't expected. I didn't want to be scared like Mom—I could see she was clutching Dad's hand—but now I was pretty uncomfortable about this flight.

The engines revved up and the plane began to speed into takeoff. As we left the ground it lurched and tilted abruptly to the right. Mom gasped. And it didn't stop. The plane kept swinging back and forth as we climbed, the engines groaning with effort. This went on and on and on, the longest turbulence I'd ever experienced. Lightning flashed outside the window. I was clinging to the arm rests, and Dad was whispering what must have been comforting words to Mom. I kept worrying something was going to happen and they'd get killed. Maybe we shouldn't have gone on this trip at all.

Now I felt guilty for putting Mom and Dad in danger—the only reason they were on this flight was to pamper me and go to the place I wanted to go. Feeling guilty made me angry. The worst part was, I didn't know who to be angry at except myself, and I didn't know how to be angry at myself. So I fixed it on Cheri Buttercup, and concentrated on what a jerk she was for bossing me around and being so evasive with me and scratching me in that horrible way.

Finally, after what seemed like forever, the plane stabilized, and I could see stars outside the window, and the seat-belt light went off. We must have passed the storm, or gotten above it. Soon after that the flight attendant came with the cart of drinks—no food on this flight, of course—and Mom and Dad both bought two of the little bottles of alcohol. I hoped it would make them feel better. If they would have served me, I might have gotten one, too, except I didn't drink.

When they announced that we were arriving at St. Calao, it was clear—we had left the storm far behind. I looked out the window but could see only a few little lights down there. I wished it was daylight, so I could see what the place looked like and how clear the water was from the air.

The landing was pretty bumpy and when we climbed down the metal steps from the plane—no jetways here—we could see why: The tarmac was just a swath of unpaved dirt cut out of the jungle. The airport was a little log building, mostly wide-open to the warm air. It was probably built out of the trees they cut down to make the airfield. The line for customs went fast because the plane was so small and there weren't many people, and the customs guy hardly looked at the passports before he stamped them. It turned out Dad didn't have to change money—they preferred dollars here, and took credit cards, too.

When we stepped out of the building I could hear drums from somewhere in the distance, and what might have been chanting. But I didn't pay much attention because we were immediately surrounded by dark-skinned taxi drivers, speaking English with a funny accent. The taxi was like an open golf cart—I guess it never got cold here. It was a short ride—the island is tiny—first through palm trees, then past what looked like just bare rock. The "resort" was made out of something like stucco, and had an outdoor restaurant next to the water, and not much else. It was a good thing we had gotten to the airport in New York early and all had fast food there, because the hotel restaurant closed at 10:00 and it was 10:30 now.

The rooms were next to each other, and I had worked it so our balconies were right over the water. The rooms were no frills, with bamboo furniture, but they had TVs and their own bathrooms. You pulled a plunger on the top of the toilet to flush it, and the shower head was at the end of a metal cable and hung on a bracket on the wall, but everything seemed clean. We were all exhausted from the uncomfortable trip, and went to bed right away. I checked the mirror. The scars on my chest were barely visible white lines.

When I woke up, sunlight was streaming through the curtains, which had a pattern of palm leaves on them. I stepped out onto the balcony in my underpants. Below me was a narrow white strip of beach and then the blue, blue sea, sparkling in the sun. The water was crystal clear; I could see the sandy bottom from my room on the second floor. We seemed to be in a cove, and in the distance I could see land curving around, covered with palm trees. My worries from the flight vanished. It was amazingly beautiful here, so different from New York in March. This was exactly where I wanted to be.

I got dressed in shorts and a T-shirt and went down to the hotel restaurant on a deck next to the water, which was protected from the sun by big multicolored umbrellas over the tables. Mom and Dad weren't there yet, and there were only two other couples eating. The waiter in a white jacket bowed when he handed me the menu. They had American breakfasts and also local foods that I didn't understand. I ordered ham and eggs and toast. I wasn't particularly hungry—I hadn't really been hungry since going to see Cheri Buttercup—but I felt I should eat since I would need the energy for the scuba certification. I was just digging in when Mom and Dad came down.

"Hey, isn't it *great* here?" I said, and forced a big hunk of toast and jam into my mouth.

Dad grinned at me. Mom tried to smile. She looked tired. She'd probably had trouble sleeping.

"The breakfast is great," I said, even though I couldn't really taste it much. Dad had what I did; Mom had tea and dry toast.

"You know, I'm not sure about this scuba business," Mom said when we were finishing. "I just feel like relaxing on the beach today. Maybe I'll go snorkeling later. But wearing a tank and swimming deep underwater—that seems kind of dangerous." She looked at me with a worried expression. "Are you really sure you want to scuba, Ken?" she asked me. "You're pretty young. I bet you can see a lot from snorkeling, and it's a whole lot safer."

Scuba diving with sharks was why I was here. "But that's the whole reason we came to this island," I told her. "And you know I'm a strong swimmer—I'm in that big pool for an hour at least three times a week."

"Well . . ." She wouldn't give up. "It's just that after that flight, I got kind of worried about this whole thing. I'd feel so much better if you didn't go deep down into the water—"

I hit the table with my fist. "A bumpy flight has nothing to do with diving." I interrupted her, trying to keep my voice normal. "That's not logical. Right, Dad?"

How could he disagree? "Well, yes . . ." he said.

"And you have to take a course and get a certificate and everything. If you don't pass one hundred percent you can't dive. It's safe, Mom." Luckily, neither of them knew about the recent shark attack. "They don't want anything to happen to people here; then they wouldn't have any business. And what other business *is* there on a place like this but scuba diving? And you have to go deep to get the bends, and I just won't go that deep."

"The bends?" Mom said. "What's the bends? I don't like the sound of that."

I cursed myself for even mentioning it to her. The less she knew about the dangers underwater, the better.

But Dad had to explain. "If you go down to a certain depth—I think it's fifty or sixty feet—and then you swim back to the surface really fast, you get nitrogen bubbles in your bloodstream. When you're down at that depth, you're at three atmospheres, so the air you're breathing has more higly compressed nitrogen in it. If you don't come up slowly enough for the nitrogen to decompress, then it comes out of the solution and forms bubbles. In the same way, if you fill a glass of water from a tap and then let it sit there, air bubbles will come to the surface because the pressure is lower. Your blood becomes like a fizzy carbonated beverage. The bubbles are too big to go through your smallest arteries, the arterioles, so they plug up circulation. It hurts like hell in the joints, which is why they call it the bends." He took a sip of coffee, then looked pleasantly at Mom. "And if the nitrogen bubbles get into your lungs they can rupture the arterioles there and cause internal bleeding, which can kill you. The only way to prevent this is to get you into something called a hyperbaric chamber right away." He slipped a forkful of egg and toast into his mouth. "So the deeper you go, the slower you have to swim to the surface, to get your body used to the change in pressure—water is heavy and there's a lot of pressure on you under all that water. That's all it is."

Now Mom looked literally sick. I wished Dad wasn't such a Discovery Channel addict. I shot him a menacing glance and then said to Mom, "But there's no reason to even go as deep as thirty feet. You don't need to go down that far to see all the different coral, and the tropical fish and all that stuff. No deeper than ten or fifteen. I promise." She still looked sick, so I added, "And anyway, I checked to make sure they have hyperbaric chambers at every diving site here, and they do." It was a lie, I hadn't checked. But I was pretty sure they had to have at least one on the island, since diving was about all you could do here.

She sighed and looked at Dad. "Do you really think it's safe?"

"People do it all the time and there are very few accidents," he said.

Mom sighed again and her shoulders slumped. If she knew I was invulnerable, she wouldn't have to worry about me, but of course I couldn't tell her. "Well, what can I do, when you're both so determined?" she said. "But I'm not getting near one of those scuba things, I can tell you that. I'm glad I brought a good, long book."

I was actually glad Mom was too scared to dive. Then I didn't have to worry about anything happening to her. Dad was stronger and a better swimmer, and knew a lot more about it, so I figured he was pretty safe.

They trained you in a small, sheltered cove that was separated from the larger one by a rope with floating plastic balls on it. They watched you: Under no conditions were you allowed to go outside the training cove until they gave you permission. I had already showed them my passport to prove I was sixteen, though I'm not small for my age. First they made you swim back and forth across the cove ten times. It was a piece of cake for me, but Dad was gasping when he finished, eleven minutes after I did. The other two couples, both American, who had been at breakfast, looked like they were only in their twenties, and they had no problems either. All the male instructors were in their twenties, too, and were built like I'd like to be.

Unfortunately, I was the only person my age, except for a local teenaged girl who seemed to be an assistant instructor. She had a hot body in her bikini, but her nose was too long and her mouth was too big and her hair was so short it was practically a crew cut, which just made her features look larger and more unattractive. She didn't even wear makeup. She was no Kaitlin.

After you passed the swimming test, they fitted you with a

miniature tank, and masks and fins. The tank was attached to a sleeveless jacket made of some kind of synthetic canvas, and padded with foam; you fastened the whole thing on with clasps around the front of the jacket.

Before you put on the mask you spit into it and added some water and rubbed it around—the spit prevented it from fogging. The mask covered your eyes and nose, and you breathed through a curved rubber contraption that fit inside your mouth, which was attached to the tank by a hose. When you exhaled, air bubbles came out of two short tubes on either side of the hose. You could feel the bubbles floating up past your ears; they made a gurgling sound. When you inhaled, there was a kind of hiss.

They told us not to take deep breaths, just to breathe normally. This was difficult at first, because the sensation was so unusual you automatically wanted to gulp in the air. And my mask kept filling up with water, which got into my nose, and also blurred my vision. This was harder than I had expected.

I surfaced and found the girl trainer, who was in a mask and big tank, keeping her eye on everybody. Other people were having problems, too, and talking to the guys. The girl fitted me with a tighter mask. "That looks better," she said. "But if you still get a little water in the mask, you push at the top like this"—she demonstrated—"so it opens at the bottom, and then you blow air into the mask through your nose. That gets the water out."

I went under again. This mask fit a lot better and wasn't leaking. I kept trying to breathe normally and finally began to get the hang of it. A little water got into the mask and I did what the girl had told me, and it worked. I began to feel more and more comfortable. But I couldn't get very deep; the air in my lungs and the tank made me buoyant, and I kept staying close to the surface. Even when I kicked hard to go down I kept popping right back up.

Now I was impatient to get the certificate and get out of this restrictive cove. But here the rules were the rules and if I tried to go too fast and skip over any steps, they might stop me from diving altogether. These instructors had sharp eyes—including the unattractive girl. It would be different after I got my certificate. Then I'd be more on my own.

Of course, I didn't even need a tank, since I was invulnerable, and I could go as deep as I wanted without worrying about the bends. But there was no way they would let me dive *without* a tank. They would stop me in a minute if I tried it. So a tank it had to be.

After about forty-five minutes of this they gave us belts with metal weights on them which we strapped around our waists, so we wouldn't be buoyant. We still weren't supposed to leave the roped-off cove, but we could at least really go under the water now. I enjoyed it more than I had enjoyed anything in weeks. It felt like flying, and the fins made you go really fast. Too bad there was nothing to see in here but sand, and other people's legs flapping around. The girl was swimming around with us to make sure nobody went past the rope, and whenever I saw her legs I swam away from them, and dove down deeper, to get away from her.

Then we stopped for a picnic lunch on the beach. They had made a grill out of an oil drum cut in half lengthwise, and cooked skewers of chicken and seafood, with a spicy barbecue sauce. The girl dished them out onto paper plates, with rice, and they had cans of soft drinks in a cooler. I sat down with my food on a log near the jungle at the edge of the beach and ate the food, because that's what was expected.

And then the girl came and sat down on the other side of the log from me. I didn't really want to talk to her, she was so homely, but maybe if I was a little bit friendly she might let me out into the real ocean sooner.

"So what's the weather like where you come from in America?" she said. She didn't have the accent all the others did; she had almost no accent at all.

"New York's a lot colder than here," I said. "We had a big thunderstorm on the way down. It could have been a snowstorm. Then we might have had some real trouble."

Her eyes widened. They were the only good thing about her face, large and very dark, with long lashes. "You live in New York City?" she asked me.

"Yeah. Manhattan. It's okay there."

"I bet it is." Her eyes gazed off into the distance. "The skyscrapers, the subway trains, the lights, the crowds, finishing high school, not having to be polite to dumb boring tourists all the time—" Then she suddenly stopped, and her eyes came back to me. "Sorry," she said. "I didn't mean to . . . to say all that. It's just that hardly anybody my age ever comes here." She laughed. "My name is Sabine."

"I'm Ken. And hey, what are you complaining about? It's so *great* here!" I said. "Never gets cold, right? You can scuba all the time. I'd rather be here in the winter than in the black slush in New York anytime."

"What's slush?" she asked me.

"It's when snow starts to melt, and it's kind of half solid and half liquid, and it gets all black with soot and exhaust, and you have to wade through it and it's freezing cold. Yuck!" I paused for a moment, thinking. "You say people our age hardly ever come here? Why not?"

"Well, mostly it's serious divers and scientists who come to this island, older, in their twenties and thirties. There's a group of them at another resort right now. People with experience. Because of the—" She stopped and put her hand over her mouth.

"Because of what? Sharks?" I whispered. Maybe I could find out stuff from her.

She was being careful. "Did you make your reservation online?"

"Uh huh."

"Well then you know, because of that warning they had to put in. But that diver was inexperienced and stupid, and got all freaked out and was thrashing around. That's what gets their attention. Somebody cooler wouldn't have gotten killed."

I leaned closer. "He got *killed*? Not just a leg bitten off or something? Where? What part of the reef was it?"

She seemed uncomfortable now, playing with her food; she probably wasn't supposed to be telling me any of this. "Farther out to sea along the reef. Farther out than we take anybody now. And deeper than we let people go anymore." She stood up. Her plate was still half full. "I have to start cleaning up and getting the rest of the gear ready." She hurried away from me.

I felt very satisfied; now I had a better idea where to go.

They told us not to go into the water until an hour after we ate, to be sure we wouldn't get cramps. That was garbage; at home I swam right after breakfast all the time, winter and summer, and never got cramps. And now that I was invulnerable, there was no way I *could* get them. So I didn't wait, and found my little tank when they were all busy with other stuff, and went right back in the water. It was much better being underwater alone, swooping and diving without other people's legs getting in my way. Too bad there was nothing to see in this dumb little cove.

And then Sabine's face appeared, looking angry behind her mask. She grabbed my arm with one hand and gestured with the other to follow her. I didn't want to, and pulled away. She shook her head in a no-nonsense way, and it hit me that if I disobeyed now, I might have less freedom later. I followed her and climbed out of the water.

"Didn't you hear me, boy? We told you not to go in for an hour," the head guy told me, frowning. "If you don't obey the rules, you don't get your certificate and you don't go diving nowhere. You got that?"

"Yeah. Yeah. Sorry," I said breathlessly. "It's just that I swim a lot at home and I never get cramps right after—"

"You ain't swimming at home now. This is your first and last warning. You do anything like this again and you're grounded."

I sighed. "Okay, okay, I promise," I said, taking off the tank. I didn't like this jerk. He had power over me, and I had to obey him, and that made me mad. But I had no choice but to go along with him and pretend to be obedient or I'd never get the chance to find any sharks or other dangerous fish.

When they let us go back in the water again they fitted us with full-sized tanks. They were really heavy out of the water, but once you squirmed into the jacket that held the tank and it was on your back, it was like wearing a fully packed backpack, which I was used to.

They were also different from the smaller ones because they had two gauges on them, attached to the tank by hoses, which floated in the water next to you while you swam. One was a pressure gauge which told you how much air was in the tank. It went from zero to five thousand. They showed us how to work an emergency valve that gave you five more minutes of air when the tank ran out, but told us we should never, never wait that long—we should always come up to get more air when the tank was still a quarter full. The deeper you went, the faster you used up the air.

There was also a depth gauge, which measured the water pressure to tell you how deep you were. The head guy taught us how to read the gauges. He told us about the bends, just about the same as what Dad had said. He explained that at the surface you were under one atmosphere of pressure, at thirty-three feet down you were under two atmospheres, at sixty-six it was three atmospheres, and so on. The more atmospheres, the more dangerous. There was only one hyperbaric chamber on the island, he said, and though the island was small it would take a while to get to it from where we'd be in our small boat out on the reef. He said the bends were incredibly painful, and they could kill you if you didn't get to the chamber in time. "Anybody who goes deeper than fifteen feet on the first day at the reef doesn't dive again," he finished. "And after that, no lower than thirty feet. Now let's go try out your real tanks."

He was probably also afraid there might be sharks if we went deeper, but he didn't say anything about that now.

Before we went in, Dad gave me a very serious look. Now he knew I had lied when I told Mom there was a hyperbaric chamber at every diving spot.

We spent the next hour paddling around in our little protected cove in the full-sized tanks. The tanks were heavy on land, but weightless in the water. After that, they took us outside the rope, where it was deeper, and let us swim around and dive a little more. Finally, we all got into a big speedboat and they took us a little farther out, where the water was choppier. We practiced entering the water from the boat. You had to sit on the edge of the boat in your scuba gear and fall off backward into the water. The reason for doing it this way was so that you wouldn't knock off your mask when you entered the water from the boat. There were six divers learning, and four instructors, including Sabine. I bet they were used to having more people.

Several people had trouble falling off backward, and couldn't get the hang of it until they tried several times. I got it perfect on my first try. It was fun, like doing a backward somersault into weightlessness. Sabine gave me a thumbs-up gesture when I came back up, grinning at me. I couldn't help smiling back at her. After all, she had told me stuff she wasn't supposed to. And she looked prettier when she smiled.

It turned out we weren't even going out to the reef until the next day. I was frustrated about that. But at the end of the afternoon they did give me a signed certificate with a stamp on it. I was now an officially certified scuba diver, and so was Dad. I could tell he felt good as we walked the short distance along the beach back to the hotel, and proud of both of us, for learning so fast—especially himself, since he was old. And even though I was frustrated, it felt good having the certificate.

Then Dad said, "No more tricks like going in the water when they tell you not to. They know what they're doing. Don't go deeper than they tell you. They know how to keep you safe. And no more lies like about the hyperbaric chamber. I won't tell Mom about it, but I don't want you making *me* worry."

I looked down at the sand. "Okay, okay."

He stopped and pulled my head around to look at him. "You mean that, Ken? This stuff is serious business."

"Yes, I mean it, okay?" I said. Then I added in a softer voice, "I really do. No fooling around. I promise." It was a lie, of course.

Mom was in a better mood at dinner. Dad kept telling her how careful and cautious they were, so she didn't have to worry as much. She'd had a relaxing day with her book, and swimming off the beach, and she loved eating in the restaurant by the sea. The seafood—which they kept saying was delicious—and the bottle of white wine they shared cheered her up a lot.

The taste of food didn't interest me. It was nourishment only.

For some weird reason I wondered where Sabine was, and what she was doing this evening. Was she at home, or was she out with friends? We had to go to bed early so we could get an early start the next day. The drums started just about when I reached my room. They seemed louder tonight.

Tomorrow we were going to the real reef. And Sabine had told me how to find the sharks. The only problem was how to get there before the instructors noticed I was missing.

As I lay in bed I thought maybe I'd be lucky and a shark would come to us. I quickly stifled that thought. I didn't want anything to happen to Dad.

The drums grew more rhythmic as I drifted off to sleep.

I'm in a graveyard at night, digging. Shadowy figures are digging next to me. The hole is deep already, and now we can see the coffin. We keep digging. Finally the coffin is free of dirt, and we jump down into the hole. Now we have tools to pry the coffin lid off. The coffin nails squeal in protest, but we keep prying and finally the lid comes off. A man in black shines a flashlight into the coffin.

The person lying in the coffin is Roger, his arms and legs twisted, his face crushed and blistered from burns.

The man in black kneels down and with his hand smears some kind of paste around Roger's ruined mouth, pushing it in, breaking off teeth, pushing it in with his fingers.

Roger's blackened eyes in the buried body blink open. He gets up unsteadily, his legs different lengths, and steps out of the coffin and stands there, hunched, as if waiting for instructions.

"The lake, the lake," people are chanting.

When I woke up I wasn't in bed, I was standing next to the window of my room, whispering, "The lake." Now I felt more frightened than I had in the dream. It had been as real and scary as the dream I'd had about being buried alive. At least I hadn't screamed this time and woken up anybody else in the hotel.

When I woke up the last time I had been screaming "Dunwich." This time I was whispering, "The lake." What did it mean?

The drumbeats danced above the gravelly washing surf.

five

We went out in the sparkling sunlight on a different boat the next morning. This one was bigger than the one yesterday, with a canopy, and an air compressor to fill the tanks. We left from a pier below the restaurant and went far enough out so that the hotel got very small in the distance. I wondered if it was farther than the thirty laps I swam in the NYU pool.

Sabine sat next to me. I didn't mind. I was getting used to the way she looked; she was beginning to seem almost cute. And she was somebody I could learn things from. "You've never really been diving on a reef before, right?" she asked me, as the boat bounced along on the glinting, frothy waves. "Ever snorkel on one?"

"Nope. I'm really excited." That was the truth, because of my anticipation of the shark. "You do the reef all the time, right? It's really beautiful, right?"

"Yeah, it's beautiful. You'll love it—they all do." *She* didn't sound excited.

"But . . . you're not looking forward to this," I said. "I can tell."

She shrugged. "It's my job. If you do something all day every day, the excitement wears off. But first-time divers are always thrilled."

It was odd. I had always longed to go scuba diving. Yet now I wasn't expecting to be thrilled—nothing seemed to thrill me anymore—except for the chance of interacting with a shark.

"This is your full-time job?" I asked her. "You don't go to school?"

She looked away from me. Now she seemed a little embarrassed, and laughed uncomfortably. "I'm sixteen. The law here says you only have to go to school until you're fourteen. So after eighth grade I had to quit. I already knew how to dive, and I was lucky to get this job. There's not a lot of places to work on this island. I'd rather do this than wait tables."

"But why do you have to work instead of going to school?" I asked her, genuinely mystified.

She gave me a funny look. "You rich American kids," she said. "My father came from America before I was born, but he doesn't have any money. My mother was from the island but she's dead now." She shrugged and looked away. "My father . . . doesn't work much. Gotta take care of him. Anyway, enough about me." She made eye contact again. "What kind of place do you live in in New York?"

I told her about our apartment, but I toned it down. I was beginning to understand. Her father was so poor, maybe a bum or an old drugged-out hippie, that his daughter had to quit school and work to support him. I guess I'd heard about people like her, but I'd never met one. I didn't know what to say. My voice faded in the middle of talking about our apartment.

Luckily the boat stopped then and she hopped up and got to work and we didn't have to continue this difficult conversation. It was hard to know what to say about her life; it made mine seem so easy, I had to admit.

The head guy went into the water first, tumbling expertly off backward, then another guy. Sabine and the third guy stayed on the boat, helping people enter the water. The two guys in the water stayed next to the boat to make sure everybody was fine when they fell into the sea. I went in last; I did it a lot better than Dad.

I went under. The breathing gear hissed when I inhaled, and gurgled from the air bubbles going past my ears when I exhaled. I was used to it now, but I couldn't help wondering what exactly would happen if I took it off.

The reef was another world from the sandy cove yesterday. I'd seen hours of underwater footage on TV, but that was nothing like really being *in* it, with brightly colored fish swimming obliviously right past your face, schools of little fish all around you, bigger ones down where it was deeper and darker.

The surface was bright above me, and blue sunlight poured down onto the reef. There was an endless variety of coral, some like huge brains, some like bright blue, unevenly knitted tapestries. There were things like long tendrils that swayed with the motion of the water, and yellow cylindrical things with spikes all over them. Tiny transparent jellyfish wafted past, long tentacles drifting behind them. I could put off disobeying for a while; I didn't have to look for sharks now. I was enthralled just exploring this alien world, so close to the one where we live, and so completely different.

I approached a narrow fish about eight inches long. When it saw me it suddenly expanded, becoming much fatter, almost spherical, and quickly swam away. A puffer fish. I had seen a show about them. They puff up like that to scare away predators. People in some places, like Japan, consider them a great delicacy. But if they aren't cooked right, or you eat the wrong part, it kills you. People die from eating them every year. It's like culinary Russian roulette. I thought it was crazy to take such a risk just for something to eat.

But for me it wouldn't be a risk. I wondered if puffer fish was on the menu here.

I popped up to the surface for a second. There was nobody in the boat now. All four guides were in the water, keeping their eyes on us. That was okay, for the time being. There was plenty to see next to the boat. And the longer I was a good boy, the more they'd relax about me, and not have to watch us as closely. Then I'd have a better chance of making my break farther out along the reef, and deeper. Back underwater I kept looking down at the big fish far below. I wondered what kind of fish they were. Certainly not anything dangerous, or they would have gotten us out of the water immediately. The economy of this island didn't need another death.

Before I knew it they were signaling for all of us to climb up a ladder back into the boat. They took us to a tiny island, just some flat rocks poking up out of the water, that wasn't far away. I couldn't believe it was lunchtime already. It was so fascinating underwater that it felt like I'd only been down there for minutes.

We sat on the rocks and had sandwiches and soft drinks. Dad and the two young tourist couples were all jabbering with excitement. None of us had ever done this before, and we couldn't get over how beautiful it was.

I was so impatient to find a shark, I felt frustrated waiting an hour before going back in. But I wasn't stupid enough to disobey them now.

Finally the hour was up and they took us on the boat to another part of the reef, farther out than the first place. "In this area it's important not to go too far away from the boat," the head guy announced before we went in. "There's plenty to see within a twenty meter radius—so stay there." And that made me realize that this must be the part of the reef where the man had been killed by a shark.

I planned my strategy. I'd stay close to the boat long enough for them to let down their guard. I'd drift very, very gradually away from the others, so they wouldn't think anything of it. And then I'd make my break and swim as fast as I could out to the real ocean where the sharks were.

It seemed to be deeper here—the coral went down as far as I could see—and I went a little deeper than before, checking my depth gauge. Below fifteen feet down, the colors gradually changed. Red faded out, and everything began to get blue. There were more fish than ever down here. It was amazing how unafraid of me the fish were, swimming right along beside me as if I were just a big harmless fish, too. Somehow they knew the divers were not predators. That was one of the things that made it really great. Only the puffer fish had been afraid.

I noticed that there weren't any legs around me now. I could see the bow of the boat far behind me and above. They were all around the boat. Nobody seemed to be paying any attention to me. I checked the pressure gauge. I had a half tank of air. This was my chance.

I turned away from the boat and started swimming as fast as I could. The long fins really helped. I didn't look back, I didn't look at the reef. I just swam farther out. I kept being afraid that at any minute somebody would grab me and pull me back. But nobody did. So I just kept going. I occasionally checked the gauge to see how deep I was. I was twenty feet down now. I went farther down.

Everything got darker and the blue deepened. What would it be like to be thirty feet down? I kept going, descending, enveloped by the darkening blue water. I checked the depth gauge. I was thirty-four feet down—more than two atmospheres.

The fish were behaving differently now. They were swimming quickly past me, in the opposite direction from the way I was going. It was like they were running away from something.

And then, in the darkness below me, I saw a very big, very pale fish over to the left. I swam slowly toward it, my pulse picking up. It turned partway around and I saw the long mouth, half open, and the rows of teeth inside, and the fin on the back. This was the real thing, all right. And it looked like it was at least fifteen feet long, plenty big enough to eat me.

My natural instinct was to get out of there fast and back to the boat. But I fought it. I knew the shark couldn't hurt me, despite how menacing it looked. I told myself I'd had plenty of physical proof already that I was invulnerable. I swam toward it faster, down into even darker water.

It ignored me.

It looked very horrible. We had learned about archetypes in social studies, and the way this shark looked was an archetype for danger and destruction if there ever was one. But my excitement was obliterating my fear now. I remembered what Sabine had said about the guy who got killed, how he'd thrashed around, how that was the way to get the shark's attention. I started thrashing, moving the water with my fins and my arms, twisting my body, trying to get it to notice me, the gauge hoses drifting around me.

And finally the shark looked up and started swimming lazily toward me, its mouth open a little wider, rows of teeth clearer. For a second I felt as though it made eye contact with me. I forced myself not to move away. And then its tail switched back and forth more quickly. It was coming at me faster now, its mouth opening wider.

I felt the water move behind me. I thrashed for real now. *Another* shark?

I looked around. It was Sabine. She had followed me. And now she was as close to the shark as I was. The difference was that I was safe, and it could easily kill her.

She gestured frantically at me in the dark water to swim back with her; I gestured at her to get away. We both ignored each other. The shark was getting closer.

And suddenly I realized how stupid this whole plan of mine was. I hadn't figured I'd be putting somebody else's life in danger. And it hit me then that I cared about Sabine.

There was only one thing I could do to protect her, and that was to get the shark interested in me. I swam toward it and stuck my arms and legs out at its mouth, almost touching it now.

That was all it needed. The huge jaws opened wide and snapped fiercely down on my left thigh.

I knew sharks didn't have a lot in the way of brains. When it found out that my leg was as impenetrable as steel, it just tried again, harder. The second time it must have hurt itself more on my body, like Adams had. It turned around and swam very fast away from me—and away from Sabine.

I swam right back to her. Her large eyes were wide behind her mask. I took her hand, and pointed back toward the boat. Its white wooden bow was just barely visible in the blue distance far above us.

It took a while to get back, slowly ascending to decompress gradually so Sabine wouldn't get the bends. I was dying to know what she was thinking. I was so relieved that she hadn't been hurt. But she had seen the shark try to bite off my leg and then cringe away. How was I going to explain it to her? And would she tell anybody?

I also felt a bond with her that I had never felt with anybody before. She had shared this momentous event with me. She had put herself in danger to help me. And she could have died because of it.

Before we got very close to the boat, near where the others were diving, I pointed up. She pulled in her hose with the depth gauge and checked it, and I did, too. We were only fifteen feet down now—no worries she would get the bends. We swam to the surface. We treaded water and took the breathing apparatuses out of our mouths.

"Are you crazy? Are you insane?" she said furiously, shaking her head to get water out of her short hair.

"I just wanted to see a shark," I said. I wasn't going to tell her the truth until I knew how much she had seen.

"But . . . it didn't hurt you. Your whole *leg* was inside its mouth and it just let go and went away. That never happens. When they start to bite, they finish." She blinked at me, her suddenly adorable brown head floating on the surface of the water. "What . . . what are you, anyway?"

I thought of the drums I heard here at night. I thought of the dreams of being buried alive, and Roger being taken out of his coffin and brought back to a kind of life. I didn't know what kind of religion they had on this island, what kind of gods they believed in.

What I did know was that Sabine lived too far away from New York, and from everybody I knew except Mom and Dad, to be able to tell them about me—and I trusted her not to tell Mom and Dad. "I'll tell you what happened. But only if you promise not to tell my parents," I told her.

"Just let me take a look first." She stuck the breathing gear in her mouth and checked around underwater, then came back up. "It's nowhere in sight. But we better get back next to the boat as soon as possible anyway. Talk fast."

"After my best friend died in a plane crash, I was afraid something like that could happen to me," I said. "And there's this old story about how if you hide your soul somewhere outside your body, nothing can hurt you. So I went to this person who had an ad that said 'Freedom from Death.' Like, a spirit woman or something. She said I had to die first, and then come back to life. She made me lie down, and I couldn't move for a while. She took my soul out of my body and hid it somewhere. And when I got home I touched something really hot and didn't get burned. A group of bigger kids tried to beat me up and they couldn't. So I knew it worked. And . . . I wanted to have kind of the ultimate thrill—to swim with a shark."

She just stared at me, her fins moving back and forth beneath her to keep her afloat—it wasn't so easy to tread water with the weights on.

"Believe me or not, that's what happened," I said, water lapping around my chin. "And you saw it. I'm sorry you were so close. I never thought I might put somebody else in danger. You aren't going to tell them about this, are you?"

"I didn't know they did it in New York," she said softly.

She kept on staring at me for a long time. She looked more scared than from the shark. "You don't think a lot, do you," she finally said, still sounding angry. "But *I* gotta think about this before I promise anything. Let's get back to the others before you get in more trouble."

"You aren't going to tell them about the shark, are you?" I pleaded with her again. "I won't do it another time. Once was enough."

"I said I'll think about it!" she snapped, and put the breathing gear back in and went under. I followed her.

It would have made me mad if anybody else had yelled at me, but not this girl. Maybe it was because she was so straightforward and honest about everything. And I knew she was right this time.

The lead guy saw us coming from underwater and gestured us to come around to the ladder back up to the boat. I went up first, the tank weighing me down out of the water, and he and Sabine followed. I was glad Dad was still underwater.

The head guy pushed his mask up. "How far away was he?" he asked Sabine.

I looked at her. It was all up to her now. She could make it so they'd never let me dive again, in which case we'd probably just go straight back home tomorrow. Or she could lie and I'd be able to dive for the rest of the week. It all depended on how strict she was about the rules—and how much she wanted to spend more time with me. And at that moment I knew I wanted to spend more time with her. I didn't care about seeing a shark anymore.

She thought for a moment. My fists were clenched behind my back. Then she said, "Not far. Not anywhere dangerous. I had my eye on him all the time. No problem."

I could have kissed her then. How could I ever have thought she wasn't beautiful? I loved the way she looked right now, standing steadily on the rocking boat deck in her orange bikini and foam jacket and black tank, her mask pushed up, dripping water. Her body had always been great, but now her face looked pretty nice, too.

"The reef is so wonderful," I explained to the guy. "I just kept wanting to see more."

"Well, it's a good thing Sabine has good eyes, it sure is, boy. If you went any farther than she thought was safe, this would have been your last dive. Nobody else wants to be a daredevil. Only you. So from now on we will *all* keep our eyes on you. You won't have a chance to get that far away again, you got that, boy?"

"Yeah, I got it," I said, feeling intense relief, even though I didn't like the way he called me "boy." Now we wouldn't have to leave the island right away. I could keep diving. And most important, I could get to know Sabine better. I wanted that a lot. I had almost gotten her killed. And she still lied to protect me.

I checked with Dad first, and he thought it was a fine idea to invite Sabine to have dinner with us that night. She was obviously a very competent and together person. I didn't have to tell him she was too poor to go to school, and probably never ate in a restaurant like the one at our hotel.

"Would you like to have dinner with us?" I asked her on the speeding boat, as it slapped the waves on the way back to the island.

"Huh?" She frowned, as if the thought of eating there had never occurred to her in her life.

"You heard me." I lowered my voice. "There's nobody else I can talk to about this. And . . . I just want to talk to you, anyway. Maybe find out a little more about you."

I'd never known anybody like Sabine. Dad already liked her, and Mom took to her right away. Mainly they were glad I had a friend here, and was really back into living again after Roger's death.

It was the best week of my life.

Sabine had seen how the shark couldn't hurt me, and she believed me about what Cheri Buttercup had done. It was such a relief to be able to talk about it, which I couldn't do at all in New York. There, it had to be a complete secret—a secret I worried about all the time. Here I could get all my concerns out in the open, with Sabine. I told her everything, though I played down Kaitlin a lot.

"You know, fooling around with your soul like that, that's a real dangerous thing to do," Sabine said. "It happens in this part of the world, the Caribbean. You've heard of zombies, people who become helpless slaves to their masters?"

"Yeah, everybody knows that zombie myth. They make movies about it."

"Well, believe me, it's not a myth, it's real—real and very, very dangerous."

Coming from anybody else, I'd think she was crazy. But Sabine was so realistic and down to earth about everything. "But . . . how can zombies be real?"

"You hear those drums they play at night up in the jungle?" she asked me.

"Yeah. What about them?"

"Those are private voodoo ceremonies, run by *houngans*. *Houngans* are voodoo priests who *don't* practice black magic. When they beat those drums, some people get possessed by spirits—I've seen it. But in other places there are *bokors*. *Bokors* are voodoo priests who *do* practice black magic. Did you notice any scratches on you after you saw this woman?"

How did she know? "Yeah. On my chest." I pulled up my T-shirt. "They're almost invisible now, white lines. Maybe you can see."

She peered closer, then nodded grimly. "She's a *bokor* all right. *Bokors* make zombies by scratching this powder into their victims. They make the powder out of puffer fish, which almost kills you, and also poison glands from certain toads. In a way you *did* die."

I didn't want to hear any of this. Not now, not in this place, with this amazing girl.

But I had to find out; that was the only way I'd have any control. "How could I have *died?*" I almost whined.

"You're still partly dead," she said matter-of-factly. "And then she gave you something else, to bring you back. It's from a plant they call zombie cucumber. They force it down the mouth. What she did to you is exactly how they make zombies here and in Haiti. And when they take their souls, they take their will, and their independence, too. I bet you didn't know about that part, did you? I can tell you'd never want your independence taken away." She paused. "Where did this person hide your soul, anyway?"

I shrugged casually, not wanting to seem worried. "I don't know. She wouldn't tell me. That was part of the deal."

Her mouth dropped open. For a moment she couldn't think of what to say. "But then . . . how are you going to get it back?"

"Why do I need to get it back? I'm safe this way. From plane crashes, from sharks, from everything."

"But I just told you. Whoever has your soul has power over you. Maybe you don't feel it yet, but you will. You gotta get it back from that woman, as soon as possible. Believe me. I'm not kidding."

"Uh . . . I had two weird dreams since this happened. Very realistic dreams. The first one I dreamed I was being buried alive. The second one I dreamed I was helping people dig up Roger's body, my friend who died—and bring it back to life. They did just what you said. A man forced something into his mouth, and then he woke up."

Sabine stared at me for a moment. "She's got you all right." She paused, and took a deep breath. "You have to understand, there are two kinds of zombies, *cadavre* zombies and astral zombies. A *cadavre* zombie is made out of the soul of somebody who really died, like your friend. It can only go where the body goes. An astral zombie is made out of the soul of somebody very close to death, who appears to be dead and usually gets buried. Then the *bokor* digs the person up and wakes him up. And the *bokor* keeps his soul, the *ti bon ange*, which has been loosened from the body in its near-death state. The *bokor* can then send the soul anywhere to do what it wants, far away from the body."

"So which kind am I?" I asked her, confused.

She looked away, and her dark skin paled a little. "I think . . . when she took your soul she made it into an astral zombie. In your dreams, your soul is telling you things, and showing you its work. The first one, about being buried alive, must have been . . . what's the word? Something that didn't really happen but gives you a clue about the situation?"

"Symbolic?"

"Yeah, that dream was symbolic, to show you appeared to be dead. But I bet the one about your friend really *did* happen, and your soul, the *ti bon ange,* was there, helping, under her control. You're going to have more dreams. Worse dreams."

"When she did that to me, she asked me Roger's name." I almost whispered. Now I felt really sick about Cheri Buttercup. I didn't want to believe it. But how else could I explain what was happening to me? There was something about Sabine that made it impossible not to trust her. She must be right about this, too. Zombies were no more unbelievable than the shark not being able to bite me, and that had really happened.

"Did you . . . did anything else happen in the dreams?" Sabine asked me. "Did you say anything when you woke up?"

"Yeah," I said, amazed. "Yeah, I did. After the first dream I said 'Dunwich.' And after the second one I said 'the Lake.' I couldn't figure it out."

"It's your soul, trying to get away from her, trying to tell you where it is." She grabbed my arm. "Pay attention. Maybe Dunwich is a place. Maybe there's a lake there. You'll have more dreams, and you'll get more clues. Pay attention. You've got to get it back as soon as possible. Things are going to keep getting worse until you do."

It seemed scarier than ever now. But what Sabine was saying also gave me a warm feeling, because she seemed to care about me in a real way.

Sabine was not as open about herself at first, but over the days and nights, as we talked more and more, she began to relax with me and tell me more about her life. "My dad." She sighed and shook her head. "He's okay. He's not cruel or anything. He's just a bum—drugs and booze, you know?" She shrugged. "It could be worse. I know kids whose fathers beat them up when they get drunk. Dad would never touch me."

"Maybe I could come over and meet him sometime," I suggested.

Her face went blank. "No," she said instantly. "Not possible."

I could see there was no arguing with her about this. It was odd.

Was she hiding something? Something about her father, or something about another part of her life? "What about your father's family?" I asked her. "Couldn't they do something to help, so you could keep going to school?"

She laughed a little. "They wrote him off when he got married to my mother. I never even met them. They probably don't even know I was ever born. So here I am, supporting him." She grabbed my hand. "Let's get back in the water." We ran across the beach and jumped into the sea. We wrestled in the splashing water, and I kissed her. The way it happened was completely natural; I didn't even think about it, it just happened.

After that, we kissed each other a lot. It was amazing, not like kissing Kaitlin. We both got lost in it. Kissing her was the only intense feeling I'd had since going to Cheri Buttercup. And my caring for her was growing more intense, too. It turned out Sabine had never had a boyfriend before. And I had never had a real girlfriend. Kaitlin didn't count.

I hadn't ever been so close to a girl. We dove on the reef during the day, and ate together and walked on the beach in the warm nights. Every minute of it was great. And it seemed like she was enjoying it as much as I was.

And I was thinking, I hadn't consciously used my power from Cheri Buttercup to get Sabine, the way I had used it to beat Adams and go out with Kaitlin. It had been an accident that Sabine had seen what had happened with the shark. Maybe that was why everything with Kaitlin and the kids at school was disappointing, because it came from Cheri Buttercup. And everything with Sabine was great, because it happened on its own.

The only thing that marred it was how worried she was about Cheri Buttercup having my soul. "Listen to your dreams, especially what you say when you wake up. That's how you'll find out where it is. If you have any problems getting it back, maybe I can help you,"

Sabine said on the beach one evening. "The *houngans* know all about stuff like that."

"But how can you help me when you're here and I'm in New York?"

"The diving company has a computer. They let me have my own e-mail account on it. You can tell me what happens and I can tell you what to do. The *houngans* will want to help me, to fight this woman you went to. She *must* be a *bokor,* someone who does black magic. *Houngans* don't like them, whether they're here, in Haiti, or in New York. Maybe . . . maybe that's what brought you to this island. Maybe the *houngans* found out about you—they can sense things from a distance—and brought you here to try to get that woman."

Again, what she was saying seemed crazy. But no crazier than the things that had actually happened.

Sabine squeezed my hand and leaned toward me. "You promise you'll do everything you can to get your soul back? Everything I tell you to do? And you'll tell me all your dreams? Do you? Promise!"

"I promise, I promise," I said, and kissed her. I'd even go back to Cheri Buttercup, if Sabine wanted me to.

The last night there we sat at the edge of the jungle on the beach with our arms around each other, wishing I didn't have to go. We were both so sad we hardly talked at all. We just held each other. The drums pounded faintly and rhythmically from the trees on the hill behind us.

Would I ever see her again?

"I'll come back someday. I really will," I suddenly said.

She put a finger up to my lips, and then rested her head on my shoulder.

The plane left in the early afternoon on Sunday. We didn't care what anybody thought and hugged at the airport, and then waved and waved. As the plane took off and circled the island—and I *could* see the ocean bottom from up here—I came closer to crying than I had in years.

And we were going back to winter in New York. And the kids who weren't my friends anymore.

And I had to make another deal with Cheri Buttercup.

six

The weather in New York sucked. It had snowed while we were gone and everything was covered with black slush. I remembered describing slush to Sabine on the sunny beach, and groaned.

Cheri Buttercup didn't sound very happy when she realized it was me who was calling her for another appointment. "What's the matter? It works, doesn't it?" she said.

"Yeah. But I've had my fun. I want my soul back now."

There was silence. "Well?" I finally said.

"I warned you it wasn't easy to get it back. But you wouldn't listen."

"Okay, so I made a mistake. But now I want it back. Can I have an appointment on Saturday, please?"

"Well, I guess it's better if I explain it all to you in person. Let me check my calendar." I waited. "I'm really busy," she said, prolonging the agony. I waited some more. "Okay. I guess you can come at two o'clock. I'll break the news to you then."

Break the news? What did she mean by that? Was it possible she would admit she'd made me into a zombie? How could I stand to wait until Saturday to find out?

The only good thing was that there was already an e-mail from Sabine when I logged on Sunday night as soon as we got home from the airport.

Dear Ken,

It was a wonderful week, the best. I think you feel the same way about it. Go see that woman and get back your soul. Tell me what happens. Tell me your dreams.

Love,
Sabine

She signed it "love." I was thrilled. I wrote her right back:

Dear Sabine,

It was the best week of my life. Everything is horrible here and I wish I was back with you. I'll call that woman tomorrow and tell you everything.

Love,
Ken

Sabine and I e-mailed every day. When I told her I had an appointment with Cheri Buttercup she said this time I should try to see more of where she lived, to get into her private space if I could, and take something personal that belonged to her. I should bring a pen and notebook and write everything down immediately after it happened, so I wouldn't forget the tiniest detail, and tell it all to her. I loved it that she cared so much.

At least it wasn't raining on Saturday, and this time I knew which bus to take. I got there early and had to wait outside her building in the wind.

Finally it was time to ring her bell. She asked me who it was, even though I could see the security camera pointing right at me. She buzzed me in.

I couldn't tell if she was wearing the same outfit or not, but it was still too short and too tight for her. Her cluttered apartment seemed more horrible than ever, after the clean openness of the island. She sat down in the leather chair and I sat on the leather couch.

"So you said you wanted it back," she began. "May I ask why you decided you don't want to be safe anymore? You did have proof that it works, didn't you?"

"Yeah, I had proof."

"May I ask what it was?"

She was more irritating than before, the way she kept saying "may I ask." I sighed. "I touched a burning-hot dish and didn't get burned. A gang of bigger guys tried to beat me up after school and they couldn't hurt me. And a shark tried to bite my leg off and couldn't. Yeah, it works all right. But I still want my soul back."

"A shark? Where were you that a shark could bite you, pray tell?"

The way she said "pray tell" so daintily made me want to barf. "St. Calao. An island in the Caribbean. We went there over spring break to go diving."

She leaned forward ever so slightly. "You meet any locals in the Caribbean?" she wanted to know. "They have some curious beliefs there—curious and misleading, I might add."

Why did she have to say "I might add?" Anyway, I wasn't dumb enough to give away anything about Sabine and what she had told me about zombies. If Cheri Buttercup knew that *I* knew she had power over me, I'd never get my soul back. I had to come up with a reason why I had changed my mind.

"No, I didn't talk to any locals," I said. "I don't know about any of their beliefs. I just went there because I wanted to see what would happen if a shark bit me. And I found out. And now I just want to be normal again. I don't like the way this feels anymore." And I was really terrified of the dreams I'd had, but I wasn't going to mention that—not yet, anyway.

"What's not to like? Nothing can hurt you. That ought to give you a lot of peace of mind."

Why was she arguing with me? Everything she said made it clearer and clearer that Sabine was right, that this woman wanted my soul so she'd have power over me.

"Look, I wanted some thrills and I had my thrills," I told her. "And . . . I don't have any friends anymore because I can't explain to them how these things happened. I just want to be a normal person again. What difference does it make to you, anyway? It's just a business transaction. You said you didn't care about having my soul. And you'll make another fifty dollars."

"Fifty dollars? You think you can get it back for fifty dollars?" And she actually laughed at me.

"But . . . but that's how much you charged the last time."

"That was one job. This is another. Different services cost different amounts. I told you it was hard to get it back."

Now I felt a chill. I hardly dared to ask her how much. I wanted to put it off. And right in the middle of the conversation would be a better time to try to get into the rest of her apartment than at the end, when she'd be in a hurry for me to leave before the next client came. "Er . . . before you tell me, I think I better go to the bathroom," I said. "All this has got my stomach kind of upset." I added the part about the stomach so she'd think I was going to be a while. That would give me more time.

She pointed. "Down that hallway. First door on the left." She lit a cigarette as I got up.

I went to the bathroom for about one second, looked at my watch, and then snuck right out and continued on down the hall, my heart pounding. I skipped the kitchen on the right, which looked completely normal. There was a closed door at the end of the hall and another one on the left side. I tried the one on the left first, praying she wouldn't catch me. What on earth would she do to me then?

It was the bedroom. There was nothing odd and mysterious about it except for her particular form of ugliness: a shag rug, a flocked pink bedspread, pillows with ruffles all over them. I quickly opened a drawer. There were rows and rows of pantyhose in it. I took a pair and shoved it into my jacket pocket and zipped the pocket shut so there was no chance the pantyhose would fall out. Less than a minute had gone by. I quietly closed the bedroom door and went to the end of the hall and opened that door.

A closet, a really big closet. It was packed with so much junk it was hard to take it all in. The first thing I noticed was the swollen carcass of a puffer fish. I recognized it because of the one I had seen on the reef. I shivered. Sabine had said they used poisonous puffer fish in the zombification powder. There were dried toads, also used to make zombies, and piles of odd charm bracelets, and things that could only be called amulets, and jars and jars of brilliantly colored powders with handwritten labels on them. There was also a doll's head, and a whip, and a staff decorated with horizontal bands of different woods. Then I saw the skulls. They were small, but they looked human. Skulls of babies?

I looked it all over quickly, so I'd be able to remember it and write it down and tell Sabine. But I didn't take any of this magical paraphernalia. One pair of pantyhose, out of dozens, she might not notice, but if anything from in here was missing it would be a dead giveaway. And Sabine had said to take something personal, not anything magical. The pantyhose were exactly right.

I went back into the bathroom and flushed the toilet and made splashing noises like I was washing my hands. She hadn't finished her cigarette when I got back, and didn't seem suspicious. I sat down. "Okay. How much does it cost to get my soul back?"

"Fifty thousand dollars," she said coolly, grinding her cigarette out as smoke poured out of her mouth and nostrils.

"What?" I jumped to my feet. "You're joking! You've *gotta* be joking!"

She patted the air with her hand. "Sit down. Relax," she said, and I slowly sat back down on the couch. Now I understood where all the jewels and the leather furniture came from. She charged a low price to give you what you thought you wanted, and a very, very high price to take it away. I had thought she was old and flabby and pathetic. In fact, she *was* evil—the only truly evil person I'd ever come across, and that included Adams, as pushy and obnoxious as he was. And she had my soul.

"You don't think I can afford to *give* my services away, do you?" she asked me. "I couldn't make a living if I did that. Most people don't believe in what I do, you know. They're not lining up outside my door, as you may have noticed. Nobody's offering me any TV contracts." She looked at her ugly pink fingernails. "I'm on my own, and I've got to take care of myself. I don't have rich parents who take me to the Caribbean over spring break, like some people . . ."

Why had I ever told her that? Why hadn't I kept my big mouth shut, for once? Now she knew my parents had money and she could charge me this impossible price.

"Look, okay, my parents aren't destitute. But popping fifty K for something like this, that they don't believe in, is out of the question. There's no way I can get my hands on that kind of money. You have to lower the price."

"I don't like it when rich spoiled brats tell me what I have to do," she said, smiling slightly. "You're in no position to tell me how much I can charge. No position at all."

"What about . . . what about if I paid in installments?" I said. That was the only way I could imagine dealing with that amount. I'd have to give up all the other things I would have spent money on—clothes, the subway, the occasional taxi, snacks after school. Most important of all, getting back to St. Calao. And it would still take a long, long time.

"You expect me to do this service in the *hope* that I'll keep getting money from you?" She smiled again and shook her head. "No way."

"What if we signed an agreement? We could make it legal and everything. I'd have to pay you a certain amount every month."

"I don't like that idea," she said, looking at her nails again.

"So there's nothing I can do? No way to get it back?"

"Fifty thousand dollars and it's yours," she said implacably.

I left the apartment in a state of total gloom. Was I going to be stuck like this forever, stuck with feeling cold about everything except Sabine, stuck with those terrible dreams that Sabine said were only going to get worse?

Cheri Buttercup had already made my soul help dig up Roger. What horrible thing would be next?

And then I remembered what else Sabine had said about the dreams: They would give me clues about where my soul was hidden. "Pay attention," she had said. That meant I would have to endure more of those dreams, and try to figure out where my soul was. And knowing Cheri Buttercup, I was sure it wouldn't be any-place easy to get to.

And then I'd have to go there and get it back myself.

Dear Sabine,

I went to Cheri Buttercup's place and told her some of the
things that had happened to me—including about the shark.
That gave away that I'd been to the Caribbean and made her
think I'm rich. I didn't tell her anything about you or what
you said about zombies, but she still said the beliefs there
were wrong. She was very nasty about everything and didn't
want to let me have my soul back. She said it would cost more
than the $50 I paid her for her to hide it.

But before she told me I checked out her apartment—I
pretended I had to go to the bathroom. I took a pair of
pantyhose from her bedroom, something personal, like you

said. There was also a closet full of magic things—a puffer fish, just like you said, and dried up toads, all sorts of charms and amulets and powders. And human baby skulls! I didn't take any of that because I figured she would notice— but she had a lot of pantyhose and probably wouldn't notice one pair.

Then I went back and she told me how much it would cost to get my soul back. $50,000! Okay, my parents have money, but I could never get my hands on that much. And she wouldn't budge, no matter what I said. She really wants my soul. And she'll keep it until I give her that money.

You said the dreams might help me to know where it is. We already know Dunwich, and a lake. That means I have to have more of those horrible dreams so that I can find out exactly where it is, and go and get it myself. I'm afraid to ever sleep again, but I have to.

Please write back soon. I really need to hear from you.

Love,
Ken

I clicked "Send." I sat back in my chair, wishing she could write back immediately. I would have called her if she'd had a phone, I needed to hear from her so much.

I did do a search for zombie cucumber, the stuff that was supposed to wake the dead, on the Web. It was a plant whose botanical name was *Datura stramonium*. When taken orally by itself it induced hallucinations. When mixed with other substances it had different effects. It was claimed by some sources that a mixture with *Datura stramonium* in it could in some cases take you out of a coma. It didn't say anything about waking you from death.

I also looked up puffer fish. The poison in them was called

tetrodotoxin. That's what killed the people who ate them. And that's what Cheri Buttercup had rubbed into my body.

I felt cold—almost as cold as I had felt in Cheri Buttercup's apartment. How much of me was alive and how much was dead?

That night I dreamed again.

I'm on the street in Queens near Cheri Buttercup's apartment. I'm carrying a knife. A man is approaching, older than me, and a lot bigger and stronger. I stand just behind a hedge next to a driveway, where he can't see me. I really don't want to be doing this, but I can't help it. I know that Cheri Buttercup has a gripe against this man, and wants him out of the way—maybe she owes him money.

He's getting closer. I know I'm supposed to stab him to death. This is worse than anything before! I can't stand to do it.

But I have no control over what my soul is going to do.

When he gets very close, I suddenly and smoothly step out onto the sidewalk with my knife. But, quiet as I am, he sees me, and reacts instantly. He kicks me hard and fast in the groin with a big heavy boot, and at the same time punches me in the stomach. This guy does *know martial arts. But I don't feel a thing. He is stunned. And now I know this is the real reason Cheri Buttercup made me invulnerable—so my soul, in my form, can kill people for her.*

He seems to know what's going to happen. He starts to turn to run away.

But now it's like he's moving in slow motion compared to me. He doesn't get a chance to turn around. Against my will, I slash his throat with my knife. Blood spurts out, splashing my face, my clothes. It's horribly warm and thick. He makes a gurgling noise and says something garbled that might be "A cave under the far side of the island." He crumples to the ground.

Then I woke up. I was standing in the kitchen upstairs, holding Mom's biggest and sharpest knife, whispering, "A cave under the far side of the island." There was blood on the knife, and I could feel more of it dripping down my chest. My heart was pounding heavily and I felt dazed.

I was very scared. And even more scared when the blood on the knife and on my chest simply faded away. Astral blood, like the astral zombie my soul was. I didn't sleep for the rest of the night. I was afraid of what would happen if I did.

I e-mailed Sabine instead:

Dear Sabine,

I just had another dream. I killed somebody—I cut his throat. I hope it didn't really happen, but I'm afraid it did. And when he was dying he said, "A cave under the far side of the island." And when I woke up I was saying the same thing. It must be a clue about where my soul is, right? Can you help me figure it out? I don't want this to happen, ever, ever again.

Love,
Ken

The next day was Sunday, so it didn't matter so much that I felt tired and achy. And when I checked my e-mail there was a letter from Sabine:

Dear Ken,

You did good at her apartment, you did exactly the right thing to take a pair of her pantyhose. That will help a lot. And I know you can do the rest too. You have it in you to get your soul back. Believe me.

Find out if somebody really got killed. Tell me. You've got

to go and get your soul as soon as possible. She's going to make it kill other people. You've got to stop it.

You have the clues now. It's in a lake in a place called Dunwich. It's in a cave underwater, probably a cave on an island. You've got to find out where this place is and go there and get it. And it sounds like you're going to have to dive.

If you have anything you can pawn—a watch, jewelry, rings, anything—sell it and buy the equipment. Run away. Leave a note to your parents telling them everything's okay, or telling them the truth. Anything so they won't worry and send cops looking for you.

Look at a map. Find Dunwich. Find the name of the lake where it's hidden. Let me know ASAP.

Love,
Sabine

Letting Cheri Buttercup get control of my soul was the stupidest thing I'd ever done. Going to St. Calao was the smartest.

I got an atlas of the United States. I started with my finger on New York City and slowly spiraled out from there. I read the name of every town on the map, big and tiny. I kept going. What if I never found it?

And then, after minutely studying the map for ten minutes, there was Dunwich. It was in the Adirondack mountains, hundreds of miles from New York City. The lake was called Lake Wannamaka, and it was too small for the map to show any islands on it. But if Sabine was right, this was the place.

I looked up bus schedules. It would have been so much easier if I could have rented a car, but I didn't have my driver's license yet, and even if I did, a car would have added hugely to the expense. I had to take a bus to Albany and change there to get to Syracuse, and then wait for hours in Syracuse to get a slow local bus that went up into the mountains to Dunwich. The whole trip would take eight hours. Then I'd have to find someplace to stay, within walking distance to the lake, if possible. I'd have to be carrying a heavy tank.

At least I could use my credit card instead of pawning things, as Sabine had suggested. That would make it all a lot easier. All that mattered was getting back my soul right away.

I wrote to Sabine and told her everything I had found out.

Then I looked up motels around the lake, online. It seemed to be a summer resort area, not a ski area, and nobody wanted to go there in mid-March, when it was still winter in the mountains, and one motel after another was closed for the season, and wouldn't open until the end of May. I didn't have that long. I had to go now.

And then I came across a Web site that looked different from the others. It wasn't a motel, it was a bed and breakfast called Trail's End Lodge. It didn't have photographs like the others, it just had little cartoonish drawings of people swimming and water-skiing and hiking. Everything was pink and blue. Everything was slightly out of focus.

The text said it was only one hundred yards from the lake. That all the breads were homemade. And it ended with the sentence, "All your needs will be met."

But the most important thing was that it didn't say it was closed until the end of May, like the others. It didn't say anything about when it was open and when it was closed, and it also didn't give a list of prices, like all the other sites.

But it did give a phone number, and their names, Tom and Jane Harding.

I was afraid to call right this minute, afraid they would be closed, too. I tried to do some homework but I was too distracted to concentrate, worrying about dreaming tonight. I kept checking my e-mail. I glanced at the Sunday paper online.

And there, on the front page, was the news that a man's throat had been slashed at 4 A.M. on the very street in Queens where I dreamed I had slashed a man's throat.

I read the story, literally shaking. The man's name was Jacob Dreyfus. He was an importer of special items from the West Indies, and had a black belt in karate. The attacker must have been very strong. There was no murder weapon, no fingerprints, and no clues at all.

My mind was a mess. I knew I had done it. There had been that weird blood on the knife last night, and on me. Sabine had said that if my soul was an astral zombie, Cheri Buttercup could send it anywhere to do what she wanted. And the fact that the murder victim imported "special items" from zombie territory was his connection to Cheri Buttercup: he got stuff for her and she didn't want to pay him.

This had to stop. Now. She was making me really kill people in my dreams! I paced the room, more worried and confused than I had ever been in my life.

It was one in the afternoon. I checked my e-mail again. Sabine had written back:

Dear Ken,

Don't wait for anything. Go to Dunwich immediately. Bring diving gear. Bring an underwater light, and a spear gun—she probably has something guarding the cave where your soul is. Do it *now*.

I wish I could go there with you!! But you can do it. Don't forget to bring her pantyhose. Wear them in the water when you go to get back your soul. And maybe you better wear them in bed at night, too. They might protect you from those dangerous dreams.

Love,
Sabine

I wished she could come with me, too! It would be so much easier if she was there, with her diving expertise and her knowledge about this kind of stuff. And it would just be so great to be with her. What would happen if I charged a plane ticket for her? Could she even afford to take the time off work?

No. I couldn't subject her to the danger. Period. I cared about her too much. She wasn't invulnerable like I was.

I had to find out if that bed-and-breakfast place was open. I couldn't put it off. If they were open it would make everything so much easier. If they weren't, it might not be possible for me to get to the lake. I picked the phone up, then put it down, then picked it up again.

I sat there holding the phone until it started making that noise that lets you know it's off the hook. I hung it up again. I had to do this now; I had to learn the bad news before I wrote back to Sabine.

I paced around my room, worrying about dates and how I would get away, and what I would say in the note to my parents. That was going to be hard. They thought I was impulsive and liked to take risks. They'd worry no matter what I told them, and probably have the police looking for me in a matter of hours.

That was when it hit me that I couldn't use my credit card for this trip—it would just make it so much easier for them to trace me. My parents had control of the credit card; they could check on what I used it for. They'd find out where I'd taken the bus and then they could check out all the motels in that area and find the one that was open—if it was open. Using the credit card for the bus and lodging would be a dead giveaway. And the fact that I bought diving equipment would make it even clearer that I was going to the lake. I *was* going to have to do what Sabine suggested and pawn some stuff to pay for the diving equipment and the bus fare and to pay these people—if they even let me stay there. There must be hundreds of pawn shops in New York, but I had never been to one in my life.

But did I even need diving equipment? Weights I would need, a light and a spear gun, too. But did I need a tank? I was invulnerable. I didn't need air underwater.

But if I *did* get my soul back, then I wouldn't be invulnerable anymore. Without a tank I'd drown. I was going to have to buy one after all.

I was still just putting off the phone call. I forced myself to dial the number. It rang and rang. They were probably closed. It was hopeless.

An old woman's voice answered.

I was so surprised I didn't say anything for a second. "Hello?" the voice said again, a little irritable now.

"Oh, hello," I said. "May I speak to Mr. or Mrs. Harding, please."

"We're not interested," she said with finality. She thought I was a telemarketer.

"I'm not selling anything," I said instantly. "I saw your Web site. I'd like to come up and stay there really soon. I know it's early . . ."

There was a pause. "Just a minute," she said, and I heard the phone clattering down onto a hard surface.

I paced around the room with the phone at my ear. She was checking with her husband. Were they open or not?

"Hello. You want a reservation *now?*" a man's voice said.

"I'd pay you extra and everything," I pleaded with him. "I just need someplace to stay near the lake, so I can dive."

"What are you talking about?" he said, sounding suspicious now. "Nobody dives at this time of year. Even in the summer people don't dive here. Waterskiing and jet-skiing, that's what they do. And those jet skis are a darned nuisance, I can tell you. Noisy. And dangerous, too. Chop up little kids. Wish they'd make 'em illegal."

I thought fast. "I don't know anything about jet skis. But I have to dive, because . . . I'm supposed to study the behavior of marine life in that area of upstate New York when the water gets cold," I said. "I'm an expert diver. And it's an important project for school. The teacher thought it was a great idea. And . . . it's going to be spring break." I figured I could get away with that. These old people in Dunwich wouldn't know when our private school in Manhattan had its spring break.

"Never heard of anyone diving here," he said.

I was getting really impatient with him now. Why couldn't he just give me a yes or no? But I didn't dare to push him much. "Diving . . . diving doesn't make any noise," I said. "And I have a wet suit, and a light to see underwater. I've been diving for years."

"You know there's a lot of snow up here. The roads are treacherous in the mountains. We only use the car to go to the market in town. And you'll have to dive under the ice. You say it's a project for school? Kind of risky for a kid, if you ask me."

Ice? I hadn't realized I would have to be diving under *ice*. Suddenly this mission got a whole lot worse. Did I really have to do this?

Yes, I had to, unless I wanted Cheri Buttercup to keep making me kill people.

"I've had a lot of experience, like I said," I told him. "Several certificates and everything."

"Well . . . all the rooms are free now. We don't usually open until May, but I can break the rules just once. Come on up. But we don't take no responsibility for this crazy diving idea. I wash my hands of it. So when do you want to come?"

I could hardly believe it. I had a place to stay on the lake! "I've got to get my bus reservations first. I'll call you back. And thank you, thank you so much. What . . . is the price for the room?" This was important. I hoped it wasn't too much, since I couldn't put the room on the credit card.

"Price? This time of year? Oh, I dunno. Depends on how much we like you. We'll decide then. Let me know when you're coming."

I said I would, and we hung up.

I wrote Sabine and told her about the incredible good luck, and how much she was helping me. I didn't want to scare her, but I told her I was going to have to dive under the ice—I had to tell *someone*.

And I looked online and saw that man did get killed. My soul really did it. You're right, I've got to go there now.

I still didn't ask her to come, even though I figured I could get away with putting a ticket for Sabine on the credit card. It wouldn't give the cops any clues about where we were going after she got here. I didn't care what the credit card consequences would be afterward. But I wasn't going to put her into danger. And why should she risk her life for me, anyway? It was my own fault I was in this terrible mess.

I just had to do this right away. Alone. I reminded myself that I would be invulnerable until I got my soul back. That made me a lot safer, even without Sabine.

I got the phone book and looked up pawn shops. There were pages of them. I started calling, starting with the ones that were closest to where we lived, to see if any of them were open today. There was no answer until I got to the tenth one. They were open until five o'clock. I had several hours.

Would Mom and Dad notice when I came back without my Rolex? I'd just have to wear long-sleeved shirts and get going before they had a chance. The Rolex was worth a lot of money. I also had a pair of very expensive dress shoes. I didn't know if pawn shops gave you money for shoes, but it was worth a try. There was also my Game Boy, which wasn't worth a whole lot, but might get a few dollars. I had $1,053 in my savings account. That was all I could get my hands on for the moment. I was hoping I could get secondhand diving equipment—I had no idea how much it cost. Tomorrow I would skip school and go to the bank and then a diving place.

Then it hit me. I was so tense and worried about this whole thing that I wasn't thinking clearly. I could put the diving gear—probably the most expensive part—on the credit card, too. That wouldn't give away where I was going—in fact, it would probably mislead them and make them think I was going south, to Florida or someplace. I just *couldn't* put on the card the bus fare and the place where I'd be staying. The bus was only $108, round trip. That jerk Harding refused to tell me how much he would charge me to stay at their bed-and-breakfast, but if I could get him to like me, it might not be too much.

I sank down into my chair with relief. It seemed like I didn't have to pawn anything after all. And the Rolex was waterproof, which might be useful.

With the credit card I could get first-rate new diving equipment. On a dive this dangerous, in dark, cold water under the ice, I didn't want to take any chances with secondhand stuff. I'd need a pressure gauge, to know how much air was in the tank. I'd need a depth gauge, too, of course, because the cave might be deep, and if it was, when I got my soul back I'd have to come up slowly in order not to get the bends. I'd buy all the equipment tomorrow and just get on the bus. It wouldn't be easy, with the heavy tank, but I had no choice.

I could relax a little more now, and concentrate. I actually worked on some homework, even though I wouldn't be going back to school until this was all over. Getting some homework done now made me feel a little normal.

In the late afternoon, just before supper, I checked my e-mail again. When the messages came on I could see that Sabine had written back. I hesitated. Now she knew my soul had really killed that man. What would she think about what I had done? Would it change her feelings for me? How could she care about a killer?

But I couldn't put this off. I couldn't put *anything* off, because of what I might dream next. I clicked on the message:

Dear Ken,

This is awful! This is terrible! You've got to get your soul back right away. NOW! Yes, that *is* the way astral zombies work. Your soul is now obeying her, taking your form and following her commands. We have to get it back before she sends it out to kill someone else.

Listen, Ken. I want to come and help you. Business is slow right now and they can give me a week off, without pay. You said you could put things on a credit card. Could you get me a ticket that way—the cheapest one possible? I hate to ask. If you can't, that's okay. But I just want to help you so much. And I miss you.

My father will let me go, though he says it's pretty cold there at this time of year. I've never seen snow, or ice.

But if you can't get away with paying for the ticket, that's okay. I can still help you from here. And from now on you *must* take her pantyhose to bed with you. It's the only thing that *might* help to protect you—and other people—from her.

Love,
Sabine

I couldn't believe it. She was *asking* to come and do this with me! It would be so much help to have her along, just for the moral support. And just to see her again. Not to mention her real diving experience.

It would also be much more dangerous for her.

For a second I wondered *why* she was offering to risk her life for me. Did she care about me that much? *Love* me that much? She must.

After all, what other reason could she have for offering to do this?

eight

I spent the rest of Sunday deleting all my e-mail to and from Sabine and any trace of the Web sites I had visited. My parents wouldn't find any clues on my computer. Then, first thing Monday morning, I took the train with my Metrocard to JFK to pick Sabine up—I didn't want to throw cash away on a cab, not knowing how much all this was going to cost. Her plane ticket was about three times as expensive as the ones I'd gotten for Mom and Dad and me, because I had bought it one day in advance instead of over two weeks. But I had no choice. We were in a hurry. When this was all over Mom and Dad could ground me and take the credit card away from me. Fine. That was nothing compared to what Cheri Buttercup could make me do *now*.

This was the first time I had ever skipped school. I was hoping my good record would mean they would assume I was sick, and wouldn't contact Mom and Dad for at least a couple of days.

I had taken Cheri Buttercup's pantyhose to bed with me the night before. I couldn't imagine actually *wearing* a pair of women's pantyhose, which Sabine had told me to do. Instead, I just held on to them, the way Mom said I used to hold on to my teddy bear when I was a baby. It took me a while to get to sleep. I was nervous about what I was going to dream, and wasn't sure the pantyhose would do any good.

I'm on a small plane, like the one to St. Calao. I have a hand grenade in my jacket pocket, big enough to blow up the plane when I pull out the pin. I know you can't take hand grenades on planes, but I hadn't gotten here by going through security. Here I am, sitting in the single seat, with a hand grenade hidden in my jacket pocket.

But the worst part is that Sabine is sitting right across the aisle from me, and she doesn't see me. She didn't see me get on the plane. And I don't try to talk to her. I don't want her to see me. Because she's the reason I'm going to blow up the plane.

I'm split in half. One part of me is watching the dream in shock and horror, thinking about the man I had actually killed in the last dream, and loving Sabine.

The other part of me wants to blow up the plane.

When the seat belt light goes off I stand up, as if I'm going to go to the bathroom, and take the hand grenade out of my pocket.

And in the next second Sabine jumps from her seat and knees me in the groin so hard that I drop the grenade, pin still in place, and fall to my knees. "Lake Wannamaka," I mumble as I go down.

When I woke up I wasn't holding the grenade, like I'd been holding the knife before; I was still in bed. The pantyhose had fallen to the floor. "Lake Wannamaka," I was whispering. That was the lake next to Dunwich on the map.

Now, at the airport, I could see that her flight had arrived. I had to wait outside security, of course. People kept coming through, and some of them looked surprised when they saw me, but just hurried on. Sabine wasn't with them. I was worried. What did the dream mean? What exactly had happened on the flight? And what were the pantyhose supposed to do, anyway?

I kept looking at my watch. Half an hour since the plane had landed. I paced around, but kept my eyes on the security area. Fewer people were coming through now. Forty-five minutes had gone by since the plane had landed. What was going on? Had she missed the flight? Had she gotten in trouble on the plane, because of the dream? Cheri Buttercup was clearly out to get Sabine now. I didn't know how Cheri Buttercup had found out about her, but I did know it was all my fault. I began to feel really sick.

And then there she was, looking hassled, and pushing a luggage cart piled high with packages. She was wearing only jeans and a T-shirt and a light jacket. I realized that it was probably impossible to get winter clothes on St. Calao, where it never got cold—not that she could afford to buy them anyway. Another expense on the credit card.

But so what? Seeing her was fantastic. I ran over to her as soon as she came through security. But her smile was tentative. And she didn't hug me as hard as I hugged her.

"What happened?" I said. "Why did it take you so long? I was so worried, because of what I dreamed last night."

"I know what you dreamed last night. You tried to blow up the plane. You were wearing the pantyhose, right?"

"I . . . I don't know. I took them to bed, but they fell down on the floor while I was sleeping."

"You must have been holding them or your soul would have blown up the plane. You need to wear them, Ken, so that won't happen," she said, her tone hard, and immediately changed the subject. "And your dream didn't have anything to do with immigration and customs." She sighed and shook her head. "My father's American, but I was born out of the country so I have a passport from St. Calao. They gave me a lot of trouble and made me wait and asked me about one million questions, and went through everything I brought with me twice. And they were rude about it, too. They got the supervisor to come in. If I was a guy I don't think they would have let me through. They kept talking about St. Calao being a third world country, whatever that means. That was a big part of the problem."

"Jerks!" I said, taking her backpack. I thought about how easy it had been to get through the airport at St. Calao. I realized then for the first time just how simple things were, in a lot of ways, for an American. And how unfair they could be if you weren't.

"Anyway, they let you through in the end, and that's what counts," I told her. "Did you check anything? We get the baggage over here."

She put her hands on her hips. "Did I check anything? Don't you remember when you came through? This is an international flight. I had to pick up all the checked diving equipment before I went through customs. How do you think we're going to dive if I didn't bring any equipment?"

"You brought your own gear?" I said, impressed and grateful. "Then I'll only have to charge one set."

"No you won't. I brought equipment for both of us. It was as much as they'd let me borrow from work, and check. One of the guys helped me with it at the airport. The only thing I couldn't bring was an underwater spear, of course—we'll have to buy that. I don't have any clothes. Only a few things in my backpack."

"You'll need new clothes no matter what. It's going to be cold up there."

"The tanks are both full," Sabine said, as we pushed the cart toward the exit. "I figured they wouldn't have air compressors in a place where it's so cold you have to dive under the ice. So we're going to have to work fast underwater, before the air runs out."

Then we stepped outside, and she instantly shrank back. "Where are we, at the North Pole?" she said, already shivering, her arms wrapped around her. "How can you stand this?"

"It's going to be worse where we're going," I said, trying to think clearly about the plans for the day. It was great that we didn't have to get diving gear. That would save a lot of time—and money. We were taking the bus tomorrow morning.

Today we had to get her a hotel room, and some warm clothes. Charging warm clothes wouldn't mean we weren't going south—she'd need them just to get around in New York. And I could charge a couple of other things for a southern climate, like a bikini and sunscreen, to set them on the wrong track.

I knew a good, inexpensive hotel on West Twenty-third Street, not far from us, and not that many tourists come to New York at this time of year, so there was a chance they had a room. But first, we had to get into the city. Again, a cab would use up a whole lot of cash. A limo would be more expensive, but I could charge it. I asked about limo service at the cab stand, and the guy got me one in about fifteen minutes. I made Sabine wait inside until it came. She had no problem about doing that.

She had clearly never been in a car like this before, and kept feeling the leather seats and studying the plush fittings.

Oddly, she didn't seem to want to talk much about the incident on the plane. All she said was "So she's out to get me now," averting her eyes but reaching for my hand. "You said you didn't tell her anything about me."

"I didn't. Not a word. All I know is what I dreamed last night."

"When you told her about the shark, did you tell her it was at St. Calao?"

"I . . . can't remember."

"Well, she's even cleverer than I thought. She found out about me. She must have contacts on the island."

"Sabine," I asked tentatively. "What do the pantyhose do, anyway?"

"Uh . . ." Sabine paused for a long moment, thinking. "Well, see, they're the human part of her, the ordinary, everyday, nonsupernatural part of her, in close contact with her. So they work against the magic part of her that is able to control your soul. It won't be as deadly when you have the pantyhose on. And they also help me to be more aware of your soul, and alert. Which I'm going to be from now on until we get it back." She didn't sound so sure of herself.

The hotel did have a room. We made it clear that we wanted a single, and that only Sabine would be staying there—we worried that if they thought we were staying together they wouldn't have given us the room because we were too young. It was great to have a place to store the diving gear. The room had a toilet but no shower—she had to share a shower with another room. She couldn't have cared less about that.

Then we went to the closest place we could find that sold warm clothes, not necessarily the cheapest. We got her a big down coat for just under $200, and a couple of sweaters and woolen shirts and heavier jeans, and a stocking cap and boots and socks. I also got some warm clothes for myself, and a small bag to carry them in. Mom and Dad would see me leave in the morning and I didn't want to look like I was going anywhere except to school. It came to a total of $420. It was a good thing I could charge it.

We went to a branch of my bank and I took all the money out of my savings account. We found a sporting goods store not too far away where we could get wet suits—they didn't have them on St. Calao. The warmest ones—the kind we had to have—were not wet suits, it turned out, but dry suits. They were made of vulcanized rubber, and came with special mittens and a neoprene hood, and didn't let any water in. The guy said you had to have them if you were diving under the ice—and wear layers of warm clothes under them, too. They were $390 each. My heart sank. I couldn't charge them, because then they would know we were going north. The dry suits took a huge bite out of my cash. But I had no choice.

The salesman said that if we were diving under the ice, we also had to have a special spool of twine that you attached to your waist. It unreeled as you swam, so the twine wouldn't get tangled, and you could find your way back to the hole through which you had entered the water. Another $20 cash gone. He said that one person should stay on the surface holding the end of the twine, so that the person diving could pull on it to signal if something was wrong. We didn't tell him we didn't have that luxury.

I bought an underwater spear gun for $200. It had one spear that was attached to it—if you shot and missed you had to pull it back and shoot again. I put a bikini and sunscreen and the spear gun on the credit card, as I had planned. The salesman seemed a little confused that we needed dry suits and sunscreen and a bikini, but of course he was glad to make the sale. When I explained to Sabine outside the store that the bikini and sunscreen would throw them off the track, she was impressed with my cunning. That made me feel good. She was usually the clever one about practical stuff, not me.

But I was still worried about cash. I only had $253 left. I would buy one-way tickets to Dunwich, which would set me back $108, leaving me with $145. If I did get my soul back, then it wouldn't matter if I charged the return tickets. But we would still have to eat up north, and pay cash for the food and for the room, because charging any of that would give away where we were. Would the money last?

I had to go home in the afternoon so Mom and Dad wouldn't suspect anything. Before I left Sabine I gave her $25 to get something to eat. That would leave me with $120 after I bought the tickets. We arranged that I would pick her up at the hotel an hour and a half before the bus left—we would have to take a cab in the traffic, instead of the much faster and cheaper subway, because of the diving gear. I promised I'd call her that night—and that I'd *wear* the pantyhose.

"Tape them on," she said. "They mustn't, mustn't come off."

It was all scary and horrible. But it was so great that she was coming with me that I could still hardly believe my luck. It had to be a good omen that she had been able to get away, and had finally gotten through immigration and customs with all that gear.

The school hadn't contacted Mom and Dad. We could get away tomorrow without me having to explain anything to them.

I kept my voice down when I called Sabine. We both felt awkward talking about how we felt, but we would have time for that later. Mainly she kept telling me to wear the pantyhose when I went to bed, and *not* to forget to bring them in the morning. I put the pantyhose on my arms and taped them to my skin, though I was so nervous and excited I doubted I would be able to sleep at all. I didn't *want* to sleep, I was so afraid of what I might dream. And all we'd be doing was sitting on the bus tomorrow. I lay tensely in bed with all the lights on, trying to stay awake.

I'm walking down a narrow corridor. It takes me a while to realize it's the hotel where Sabine is staying. In my pocket I have a Ziploc bag containing a wad of cotton soaked in deadly poison. One breath of it will kill Sabine. Again, I am horrified about what I'm going to do. But I can't stop. Part of me hopes Sabine barricaded the door. The other part of me knows I can get in, even if she has.

I stop at the door of her room. I reach into my pocket and pull out a skeleton key—I don't know how I got it, but, like the knife and the grenade, it is here at my disposal. I fit it into the lock. The door opens easily and silently.

There are no lights on in the room, and the Venetian blind on the window is closed. And yet I can see everything very clearly—in this form I have per-

fect night vision.

   Sabine sleeps in the narrow bed. Part of me is awed by how lovely she is. The other part of me moves toward her silently, taking the cotton out of the bag. Sabine sleeps on her back, her head to the side on the pillow. It will be easy to hold the cotton over her nose as she breathes.

   Just before the cotton reaches her, she kicks out at my gut with both feet. Her legs are strong, and she kicks really hard. I fall back onto the floor, gasping, the breath knocked out of me again. Something fuzzy floats in front of my eyes, a glowing blue light. I'm groaning, "The Blue Lantern."

And then I was awake in my own bed, mumbling "The Blue Lantern." This time I *was* still wearing the pantyhose on my arms. Why weren't they preventing the dreams? And if they weren't working, how could Sabine fight me?

It was getting light out. I decided not to sleep any longer—there would be plenty of empty time to sleep on the bus, where Sabine would be safer. And before I did anything else I put the pantyhose in the backpack I carried every day, to be sure I wouldn't forget to bring them with me. I also brought the roll of tape.

I put a note on my desk that said I was on an important errand and not to worry about me—I'd be back in one or two days. They wouldn't look in here until late afternoon or dinnertime. By that time we'd be in Dunwich.

I left the house at the usual time for school and Mom and Dad acted completely normal. I hoped I did, too. I took the subway up to the hotel, only two stops away. Sabine was waiting for me in the lobby with all her gear when I got there. She didn't smile when she saw me. "Good thing you were wearing the pantyhose last night," she said. "You have them with you, right?" I nodded. We didn't say any more about me attacking her in the hotel.

We still had a little time so we checked our stuff and got Sabine breakfast. As she ate, I told her how I had dreamed the words "Lake

Wannamaka," and "the Blue Lantern." We already understood what Lake Wannamaka meant. In Dunwich we'd have to keep our eyes open for a blue lantern, or anything with that name.

We got a cab, which crawled to Port Authority bus station. I kept looking at the meter. The cab fare was $12, including a very meager tip, so the driver didn't help us at all with the gear. The fare would leave me with $108 after I bought the bus tickets.

Port Authority bus station was full of bums and crazies, as usual. Some of them were huddled on the floor with plastic bags holding all their possessions. One old lady with long gray hair was reaching her frail arms out at people hurrying by.

Sabine kept looking back at them as we passed. She put her hand over her mouth when I told her they had no place to live. She told me they didn't have homeless people on St. Calao. If you didn't have any money you could build a tin shack—up in the jungle, away from where the tourists could see—and it never got cold.

Scared as she was about how Cheri Buttercup had tried to murder her two times in a row, she seemed genuinely moved by the plight of homeless people in New York in the winter. I had never thought about them much, but now I sort of knew what it felt like not to have enough money. Being with Sabine was changing the way I felt about a lot of things. I wondered then what kind of place she and her father lived in. I already knew they couldn't even afford to have a phone.

I had called the bus line yesterday. I couldn't buy or even reserve a ticket without going there in person because I didn't want to use the credit card and give away where we were going. But they had assured me that this bus was never full at this time of year, so I hoped we could get a ticket. I had called Tom Harding and told him a friend was coming too, and hoped that was okay. I didn't mention that it was a girl and that she was half Caribbean. I told him what time we would arrive in Dunwich, and asked him how to get to his house. He said he'd pick us up at the place where the bus stopped, which was right at the market where they bought their food anyway. That was good—it would save some cash.

There was only a short line for the tickets, but I started to get in front of everybody else anyway—it *had* to be more important for us to get on this bus than any of these other people.

Sabine pulled me roughly back to our place. Everybody looked. "Don't be a jerk. Wait your turn," she admonished me. "The bus has got to hold more people than this. Save your aggression for fighting that woman."

We had no trouble getting the tickets. Sabine said it was a sign that luck was on our side.

I wasn't so sure. Now we only had $108.

But I took her hand and said, "I'm lucky because you're coming. You're an expert diver. I don't think I could do it without you."

She shrugged. She looked so different all bundled up in her winter clothes, smaller somehow. "Yeah, I have a lot of experience diving in clear, sunny, warm water on St. Calao. I've never been in dark, cold water under the ice." She grimaced and shook her head. "We're both just as inexperienced with that. And we only have one tank of air each and can't refill them, I'm sure. I don't see how it could be worse. That's why I know we're going to the right place."

We put all the big stuff underneath the bus and our little bags fit easily above the seats. We didn't get the very front seats, next to the driver, which had the best view, but we got the ones right behind them. I insisted Sabine have the window seat. It took a long time to get out of the city, through all sorts of poor, ugly, bleak neighborhoods, before the highways got going, but Sabine was still fascinated—she had never seen a city anything like this big before. And once we got into the country she was still fascinated by the pristine, snowy fields, and the trees with icicles all over them. I dozed off a lot, without dreaming. Whenever I woke up, she was still staring raptly out the window.

The Albany bus station was small and ugly and cheap. I got Sabine a sandwich and a drink—I was never really hungry anymore—for $8, which left me with $100. She saved the sandwich for the bus to Syracuse, which left in half an hour. Out here it was hillier and I could appreciate the winter scenery, too. We didn't talk a lot. I could feel that Sabine was as worried and scared as I was, but she didn't want to admit it. On the Syracuse bus we sat in silence, though Sabine commented on how good her sandwich was—she had never had corned beef before. I wanted to tell her it was usually much better than that, but decided not to, so she'd enjoy it more.

The Syracuse station was a lot nicer than Albany, bigger and more modern with more comfortable places to sit. That was good. It was two hours before the bus for Dunwich left. I spent $10 on a couple of magazines that interested Sabine, which left me with $90—I had brought a book. It all might have been fun, an adventure, if we weren't so worried about what was ahead of us. We both knew without saying it that we had to make the dive tomorrow.

The bus to Dunwich was old and rickety, more like a city bus, not streamlined like the others had been. The seats were plastic, not plush, and did not push back, so they were a lot more uncomfortable. There were only about six other people on it besides us, and we got the very front seats.

We'd been on divided highways until now. The road to Dunwich was a two-lane road going up into the mountains, with lots of curves and steep stretches. Some patches of the road were icy, and the bus had to go slowly. There were very few towns, mostly pine forests on both sides of the road. We also passed occasional bare patches of land where we could see mountains in the distance, and frozen lakes. Sabine was even more fascinated now.

The chilling winter scenery and the hills and frozen lakes just made me want to be gloomy. Then I would remind myself that I was sitting next to Sabine, and it was like cold boots being warmed beside a fire.

I hoped I could avoid killing her.

It was just about 5:00 and almost dark when the driver called out "Dunwich," and pulled the bus up beside a small brick market. Then it hit me—how were we going to recognize the Hardings?

"We don't know what they look like," I said to Sabine as we got our stuff down from the overhead rack.

She looked back. "It doesn't seem like anybody else is getting off here. So they'll be the only ones meeting the bus."

I remembered that I hadn't told Mr. Harding that Sabine was half Caribbean, in case they might be racist. What if they were? What if they didn't want her to stay in their house because of her color, or didn't want us to stay together because we were young? Who knew what dumb ideas people living in a place like this might have? We climbed out of the bus into the gathering darkness. The driver opened the compartment underneath and we got out all our gear. We had to wear the tanks on our backs; they were heavy and it was easier than carrying them. We looked around. Nobody was waiting where the bus had stopped.

"You kids okay?" the bus driver was nice enough to ask.

"Sure, sure," I said. "They'll be here to meet us."

He lifted a hand, climbed back into the bus, and drove away. We stood by the side of the road. This was the center of town, but there were only a few buildings on either side of the road, and then nothing, scattered pinpoints of light way off in the distance.

I kept looking for a blue lantern, or something with that name, but didn't see anything.

I knew Sabine was wondering if they would show up, too, but I didn't say anything about how worried I was. I wanted to come across as strong and tough. The one motel I saw was completely dark, the neon light unlit, obviously closed. The street was almost completely empty of pedestrians. It was also a lot colder up here than in the city. The only activity was the few people going in and out of the market. They all ignored us.

I couldn't help looking at my watch. 5:15. I had told him we arrived at 5:00. Fifteen minutes wasn't very late but in only a few minutes it would start to get serious. Maybe we could ask at the market if there was anyplace open where we could stay. How long should we wait before doing that?

"Sabine," I started to say. "Maybe we should . . ."

An old station wagon pulled up and stopped right in front of us. The window rolled down and an old man leaned over to us from the driver's seat. "Pritchard?" he said. "It must be you, with all that gear. Come on, get in, it's cold out there. You can put your stuff in the back first. I made sure it was unlocked."

I had been prepared to show him my credit card and other I.D., such as Sabine's passport, to prove we were really who we said we were, but he didn't seem to want to see them. I opened the back of the station wagon and we put in all our gear and our two bags. Then I got in front and Sabine got in the back seat. Harding gunned the engine and jerked to a start. He hardly looked around for a second before pulling out into the road. Then he was going a lot faster than the bus driver had.

"Nice to meet you, boy—and girl." He glanced at Sabine in the rearview mirror but it was probably too dark for him to see what color she was.

He was driving much too fast on the curvy, icy road, and he kept looking at Sabine in the rearview mirror. Every once in a while the car would skid and he'd have to suddenly jerk the wheel to get out of it. I felt like Mom on the plane, gripping the hand-rest on the door, even though I knew nothing could happen to me.

"So who are you?" he asked Sabine.

"I'm Sabine Shearing. A friend of Ken's. We met in the

Caribbean, where I'm from." She didn't sound very comfortable about being in this car, either, but we didn't know this man at all and so couldn't correct his driving. "I'm a diving instructor and guide on St. Calao."

"The Caribbean, eh?" he said, and laughed. "Well, I've never been there. But I can tell you one thing. It ain't nothin' like that around here at this time a year. Hope you can get used to it." He jabbed me in the ribs with his elbow. "And you, too, young fellow. Oops!" he added, as he almost skidded into an electric pole.

Now I was almost as worried about just getting to their house as I was about making the dive the next day—and going to sleep tonight.

nine

Unbelievably, when we turned off the main road into the woods, I saw a wooden building on the corner with a sign that said "The Blue Lantern." It was an amazing coincidence that the Hardings lived on a road that had a landmark I had dreamed about.

It seemed to be a gravel road because of the noise of the tires on the surface. Snowdrifts were higher than the car on either side. After about a hundred yards, Harding pulled over to a house on the left, where there was a tunnel dug in the snow drift to get to the path to the door. There were no other lights around.

"This your place?" I asked him. "Pretty isolated."

He waved his arm. "Oh, there's other inns and houses around the green and down toward the water, but they're all open only in summer, can't see 'em now. We're the only ones who stay here all winter—and this is probably the last winter we're going to. Getting too old for this. You're the only guests we've had since October. And the town doesn't like plowing the road just for me."

Maybe that was another piece of luck for us, that they had decided to stay the winter one more year.

We stepped outside the warm car into the stinging cold.

"You're going to have to bring your stuff in yourself. My back won't let me carry that kinda stuff anymore."

"How far down the road is the lake?" I asked him. We quickly began to unload in order to warm up.

"Oh, not far. The pier's about a hundred yards away. Don't know how deep the ice is. People come here and fish through the ice in the winter. If you're lucky there'll be a couple of holes already." He shook his head. "Your folks know you're doing this, diving under the ice?"

"Yes, yes!" we both said quickly.

The house was made of big gray stones, with a long wooden porch across the front. Sabine and I lugged our stuff into a living room which also had stone walls and big old couches and pictures of sailing ships. Beyond it was a dining room with several tables, open to the living room, and on the other side of that some glass doors that might lead to a deck. I guessed the kitchen was to the left of the dining room—I could hear pots clanking in there. For Sabine's sake, I was hoping they'd be nice enough to feed us dinner, even though it was just a bed and breakfast, because there hadn't been an open restaurant between here and the market.

"Master bedroom's down here—the missus and I don't like to use the steps too much at our age," he said, pointing off to the left. "We have help in the summer when there are guests all the time. Your two rooms are upstairs, the first ones to the left and right of the stairs. And notice I said *two* rooms," he added, squinting at me.

"No funny stuff goes on in this house. And if you're smart you'll carry up all your gear right away—the missus don't like a lot of clutter."

Then he turned and got his first good look at Sabine in the light. "Oh, so you're a native girl, I see," he said, and winked at me. "Well, takes all kinds." I didn't know what he meant by that, but at least he wasn't kicking her out. "You ever been this far north before? Ever seen snow and ice?"

"Never." She shook her head. "It's amazing."

"Amazing?" He laughed. "Wait'll you get in the water under that ice."

We lugged our stuff upstairs. There were several bedrooms, pine paneled, with windows under the eaves. Sabine picked the one on the right of the stairs so I went on the left. There were two big bathrooms but we decided to share one.

"Hey, I think this is the very same road my soul told me to look for," I whispered to Sabine before we went back down. "There was a sign that said 'The Blue Lantern' when we turned off the main road. Remember, I told you I saw that in my last dream."

Sabine lifted her hands. "Like the *houngans* on my island say," she said. "These things fit together." She looked hard at me. "But it still doesn't mean it's going to be easy."

As if I didn't know.

Harding had a fringe of white hair and a big gut, and wore a plaid woolen shirt. He gestured at us to come into the kitchen. A plump, elderly lady with curly white hair was just closing the oven. She wiped her hands on a clean, checkered apron and smiled before shaking mine. She did seem a little surprised when she saw Sabine, but she covered it up right away and shook her hand. But I knew Sabine had noticed. What did it feel like to have people react to you like that?

Mrs. Harding wasn't as talkative as her husband—all she said was hello. "Stew smells pretty good," Harding said. "Nothing like stew on a night like this. Don't be shy about eating as much as you want. You two got a tough day tomorrow."

Sabine seemed to be letting me do most of the talking; it only made sense, since I was from around here. "We . . . weren't expecting you to have to cook dinner for us," I said to Mrs. Harding. "This is a bed-and-breakfast place."

Mr. Harding guffawed. "What'd you expect to do, bring your own sandwiches and picnic on the lawn?" he said. "Ain't no restaurants for miles and miles at this time a year. Don't worry, we'll add it to the bill." He laughed again. "Time for me to set the table, dearie?" he asked his wife.

She smiled shyly and nodded.

"That's my job—this time a year, anyway," he explained to us, opening a cupboard.

We sat at the biggest table in the dining room. The beef stew had carrots and sliced onions and boiled potatoes in it. There was also soft white bread, and a salad of iceberg lettuce and hard pale tomatoes and a bottle of ranch dressing with fake bacon bits. Mom would have disdained the salad, but I could tell Sabine was grateful for every bite.

And what were Mom and Dad doing right this minute, anyway? Had they called the cops? Were the credit card expenses online yet?

"It's . . . it's really nice of you to take us in like this, out of season," I said as we ate.

Harding waved his hand at us and then finished chewing a bite of stew. "I trust you kids. I got instincts. Anyway, if you were any kind of crooks, you wouldn't be wasting your time up here, now, would you? And it's nice to have young folks around at this time a year. Gets kinda lonesome sometimes. Another reason we probably won't stay up here another winter."

And it struck me again that there was something a little odd about how welcoming he was, when they were supposed to be closed to guests, and he knew absolutely nothing about us except what I had told him over the phone. He wouldn't even discuss a price! You'd think he would have made sure we could pay, and checked with my parents about what we were really doing here, and if we had their permission to do something as dangerous as diving under the ice, or at least looked at Sabine's passport. Why was he going out of his way to be so nice to us? Just because they were lonely?

I couldn't figure it out and now I needed to discuss it with Sabine. It just all seemed too easy, somehow. Sabine would have a good take on it, I knew that.

"So you come from the city?" he asked me.

"Yeah. We live in the Village."

"I know this is a crazy question, the city's so big," he said, and laughed at himself. "But you wouldn't happen to know a lady who lives there named Cheri Buttercup, would you?"

I choked on a bite of stew, and could feel Sabine's eyes on my face. "Cheri . . . Buttercup?" I managed to say.

"I knew it was a crazy question," he said.

Sabine and I were avoiding looking at each other on purpose. I wished I knew what tack she would want me to take about this. "Cheri Buttercup?" I said again, stalling for time.

"Yeah. Just a lady who comes here in the summer, sometimes."

But actually, now that I'd had a little time to take it in, it didn't seem so odd that he would have met her. She would have had to pinpoint this place exactly before she could hide a soul here, wouldn't she? It wasn't *necessarily* suspicious that he knew her.

"Funny coincidence," I said. "I went to her place—to ask her about a friend of mine. You know what she does, right?"

He laughed. Why did he have to laugh so much? It was beginning to seem artificial, like he was covering up some other emotion. "She's one of those whatchamacallits—claims she has 'special powers' or something. So she says. She stayed here once, but now she stays in a motel down the road. But she likes the beach here and she pays for the sticker to park. Funny coincidence, all right, you going to see her." He peered closer at me in a way I didn't like. "You say you went to ask her about a friend?"

I didn't want to talk about Roger. Death—my own, Sabine's, Roger's—was on my mind too much of the time now. "A friend of mine who died. It's one of the things she says she can do," I lied— she had never claimed to be a psychic. "Communicate with people on the other side."

He waved his hand in a put-down kind of way. "A good, normal kid like you. You don't believe in that kind of—" He started to say something, then changed to what was probably a more polite word. "That kind of stuff, do you?"

"I was just upset about my friend, and she was in the phone book. I think she guessed a lot. But she knew some stuff, too."

"She send you here?" Harding asked abruptly.

Sabine dropped her napkin on the floor. "Oh, excuse me," she said.

I knew she was telling me not to say too much. "No, no, just a coincidence that you and I both know her," I said quickly.

There was homemade apple pie for dessert, with cheese. Sabine had never had pie before, and didn't want a second piece. Harding offered us coffee. Sabine declined, but I didn't know what to say. I knew I should probably sleep, because we had a tough day tomorrow. But it would be safer if I stayed awake—I was afraid of what I would dream. So I had a cup, though I doubted caffine could affect me anymore. We excused ourselves after dinner, saying we were tired from the trip, and had to get up early, as soon as it was light.

"Sure you don't want to watch some TV?"

"No, thank you." I faked a yawn. Sabine and I needed to have a talk, alone. It was a good thing the Hardings didn't like to come upstairs.

I closed the door of her room and sat down on the wooden chair across from her single bed. "So?" I said.

"I better get a lot of sleep. We're going to have to work fast tomorrow."

"I know that. But I mean—these people, this place. Doesn't it seem a little *too* convenient?"

"These things work out like that. And tomorrow isn't going to be convenient at all. I wonder how thick the ice is. We won't be able to see much. We're going to have to know exactly where the hole is, how to get back to it when we have to surface. Even with the spool of string we got, that's going to be real tricky."

I held up my hand. "Wait a minute. What do you think about him knowing her?"

"I don't think it means much. She'd have to come here in order to know where to hide it. She'd have to know the exact place, precisely. I think she'd even have to go to the place herself. That may be a good sign. She's older and we're in a lot better shape than she is, from what you say. If *she* could get into this underwater cave, then it ought to be pretty easy for us. Except for the ice. She came here in the summer, of course. And once she'd been here, she could send souls on their own anytime."

"But what if he's on her side? Under her control or something? He laughs too much. He didn't check up on us or anything or want to talk to my parents. I think most people would do that. It makes me suspicious. Maybe he's . . . like me. But farther along, more under her control."

"*That* guy? A zombie?" She said it as though I were nuts.

I wanted to believe her. I noticed there was a bolt lock on her door. "Be sure to lock your door when I go to bed," I said.

"I sure will—but not because of him." She let that statement hang in the air for a moment. "You know, Ken, as much as I care about you, I'm also scared of you. That changes things. We've got to fix this by tomorrow. Come on. Exactly what are we looking for underwater?"

"All I know is an underwater cave. It must be in an island. We should have asked him about an island. If we're lucky there may be some holes in the ice around it already, from fishermen. He said people do ice fishing here."

"If the ice is strong enough we can just walk out to the island and not have to waste any air getting that far," she said.

"Great idea." I wished I'd thought of it.

"*If* we get into the cave, *if* we get past whatever guardian or trap she put there, and *if* we find whatever she put your soul in—usually it's a bottle—don't open it," Sabine said. "If you open it she'll know you got it back—and we'll be better off if she doesn't know."

"But if I'm not going to get my soul back, then why do I need to wear all this gear? I'll be invulnerable all the way to the cave and back."

"Because just holding on to the container of your soul might make you vulnerable again. I don't know exactly how that part works." She sighed. "It could be easy—or it could be impossible. Weird, how I got into this kind of thing in a place like this."

"You're not going to back out now?" I said, suddenly really afraid.

"No, no. Not after we went to all this trouble and all the money you spent. I just hope we make it." She lowered her voice. "And before that, I hope we—I—get through the night. I'm glad you had that coffee. But tape on those pantyhose tight in case you go to sleep."

The door burst open and Harding stomped in, shaking a finger. "I could hear you coming in here from downstairs, I'm not dumb," he said, and leaned back and laughed. "I waited a bit to see what you were going to try to do. Good thing for you all four feet are on the floor. That's the rule in this house for kids your age. I thought you said you wanted to go to bed early."

"We do, we do," I told him. "We just—had to make a few plans for tomorrow."

"Well, make 'em tomorrow. Time for you to go to bed."

"Is there an island anywhere near here?" I asked him.

"Yeah, a little one, about a hundred yards to the left of the pier."

"You think fishermen ever dig holes in the ice there?"

"I don't spend my time sitting out in the cold watching where they fish," he said unhelpfully.

I thought of something. "Oh, could we borrow a shovel or an ax or something in case we have to dig a hole?" I said. "That's the only gear we forgot to bring."

"I got a pickax and a shovel I can let you use—just be sure to bring 'em back. Come on, young man. Off to bed now." It was almost as though he didn't *want* us to have a private conversation.

We took turns showering before going to bed—it had been a long ride and we didn't want to waste the time in the morning. It was an old-fashioned shower and Sabine had trouble getting the water temperature right, and I had to help her, and Harding came up again to check on what was going on. After we got rid of him we both took our time brushing our teeth and all that. I had the distinct feeling that Sabine, like me, was actually putting off going to sleep. If things worked out tomorrow, this would be the last night Cheri Buttercup would have any control over me. If she had any sense of what we were doing, we both knew she would certainly try harder than ever to get me to kill Sabine. I hoped the coffee would keep me awake. Even if I was tired tomorrow, the adrenaline would probably keep me going.

Sabine very carefully taped Cheri Buttercup's pantyhose to my arms. She used more than twice as much tape as I used the last time, and wound it around the pantyhose down to the wrist. We wanted to be sure nothing could get those pantyhose off me.

Of course I was nervous and alert. I'd slept on the bus, so I didn't feel sleepy now. That was good. I hoped the coffee would keep me awake and I wouldn't sleep at all. I kept checking my watch.

But gradually my eyelids grew heavier and heavier . . .

And now I know that I'm right and Sabine is wrong. Because in this dream I'm not stalking Sabine alone.

Mrs. Harding is working with me.

ten

I get out of bed with my knife and unlock the door of my room and Mrs. Harding is standing right there. Her hair is in curlers under a frilly plastic shower cap, and she has on a ruffled pink bathrobe. Over the bathrobe she is wearing the same checkered apron she was wearing that evening. A serrated bread knife and a large carving fork poke out of her apron pocket.

We both have that special night vision.

I'm two minds fighting again. One part is desperate to save Sabine. The part of my mind that's under Cheri Buttercup's control just wants Sabine dead.

We walk quietly past the stairway to the door to Sabine's room. No skeleton key can unlock this dead bolt from the outside. "How are we going to get in?" I whisper. "I know she locked the dead bolt. No key will get in. And what about your husband? Won't he miss you?"

"He's dead to the world. Anyway, we don't need him." I didn't notice before how high-pitched her voice is—or maybe that's just because she's in her zombie form. She giggles. "As for that lock—one of my clever little tricks we should all know about." She pulls the carving fork out of her apron pocket and wedges it into the edge of the door. She fiddles around with it, her tongue just poking out from her teeth. In a minute or two the bolt slips loudly open.

"But that will wake Sabine," I say. "She'll be prepared."

"She's no match for the two of us." Mrs. Harding laughs, a sweet little tinkle, and pushes open the door.

The bed is empty.

We look silently around the small room. It has a wooden chest of drawers and the one chair, and nothing else. And Sabine isn't there.

"Impossible," Mrs. Harding mutters. "The bolt was locked, on the inside of the door. She couldn't have gotten out and then locked it from the outside."

Then I know that Sabine is under the bed. I struggle, and manage to stop myself from telling Mrs. Harding. I also notice that the window is open. Sabine wants her attacker to think she jumped. We run to the window and look out. We can see footsteps in the snow just below the window. How could she have done that and then gotten back inside? She's clever, all right.

"The little dear actually jumped," Mrs. Harding says. "Well, she won't get far in this weather. And we're impervious. Come on!"

Why doesn't she know Sabine is under the bed, the way I do?

I'm having a terrible battle with myself. One part of me—the part that loves Sabine—wants to let Mrs. Harding run outside and lock her out and get rid of her. The other part of me—the Cheri Buttercup part—wants to tell Mrs. Harding Sabine is under the bed, so we can attack her together.

But I haven't even gone for Sabine yet. My soul is fighting Cheri Buttercup better than ever.

Mrs. Harding starts for the door. Then she stops. "No. That sweet little jungle bunny wouldn't be hiding out there in the cold with her thin, southern blood," she says. "I know where she is. If you know cooking, you know how to think. And I can tell she's not a cook." She moves toward the bed.

A long pole that I know is the spear gun sweeps out from under the bed and knocks Mrs. Harding in the ankle. She's plump and not too steady on her feet, and over she goes, dropping the carving fork. But she still has the bread knife. For a moment she just lies there on the floor, stunned. I start crawling under the bed with my knife to get Sabine.

But Mrs. Harding is still in front of me. She pokes her head under the bed and lashes out fiercely with the bread knife.

I hear Sabine cry out in pain. Mrs. Harding lunges again.

Sabine swings out farther with the spear gun. It has a mean point, but Mrs. Harding rolls out of the way. It must be just an instinct, because of course nothing can really hurt her.

Now's my chance to get Sabine with my knife. I kick the spear gun out of the way.

But in the second before I go for Sabine, the small remaining sane part of my brain takes over. I kneel down and hold my arm, which on my body in bed is covered with the pantyhose, on Mrs. Harding's back as she lies there, momentarily dazed, holding her bread knife.

At the same moment, Sabine kicks Mrs. Harding in the gut.

And then she's gone.

What made her go away? The stocking, or the kick from Sabine?

Sabine's hand shoots out and grabs the spear gun and lashes out with it again. It knocks the knife out of my hand as she kicks me.

And I was sitting up awake in my own bed. Outside the window the snow glowed a lovely orange and pink.

eleven

"The missus had a little fall last night. Hurt her ankle. I'll call the doc when he opens up in a couple hours. So I'm gonna have to do your breakfast. Luckily, it's the only things I can make—sausages and flapjacks with plenty of butter and syrup. Just what you need."

Of course Mrs. Harding was faking it, for some reason—nothing could hurt her. Mr. Harding's food sounded pretty heavy, but he was probably right. The fat and carbohydrates would give Sabine energy and keep her warm—I'd heard Eskimos ate a huge amount of blubber.

We had been very lucky last night that Sabine had survived, with Mrs. Harding joining up with my zombie soul. If things worked out today—and it was a big if—that was the last attack.

And because Sabine had been awake, she knew that Mrs. Harding had been the main attacker, not me, as before. Luckily she had been crouching so far under the bed that Mrs. Harding had only been able to scratch her superficially with the knife, she told me upstairs. I couldn't see it because she was fully dressed.

We were in a hurry in the morning and didn't have much chance to talk, but at the top of the stairs Sabine said, "You're a pretty strong and stubborn guy to be able to fight off the zombie commands like that." And she kissed me. That made what we had to do today seem a little bit less impossible.

It seemed pretty clear that Mr. Harding didn't know anything about his wife's zombie nature. And I had suspected *him!* Lucky for us they weren't both that way. If he had been fighting, too, I didn't see how Sabine could have lived through it.

It had to have been Cheri Buttercup who had done this to Mrs. Harding. She probably didn't use her very much. What errands did she need done for her up here? I couldn't imagine *Mrs. Harding* being the one to hide my soul—though she had been tougher last night than I would ever have expected. But why had Cheri Buttercup made her a zombie, anyway? Had Mrs. Harding, like me, come to ask her to be made invulnerable, without understanding the consequences?

The pancakes were doughy and leaden, and the sausage patties glistened with grease, but we both ate a lot. Maybe it would help me . . . at least when I had my soul back.

"I'll give you a lift down to the pier so you won't have to carry all that equipment," Harding offered. He really did have a big heart. I felt guilty for having been suspicious of him. He remembered to throw a pickax and shovel into the back of the station wagon.

"Could we borrow something else?" Sabine asked him. "We don't want to get lost under the ice. We have a spool of twine, and we need to nail the end of it next to the hole. But we don't have a hammer and nail."

"Good thinking, girl. I'll be happy to let you have them."

After breakfast we went upstairs. Sabine cut the pantyhose in half and we each wore one leg on our arm. We put the dry suits on over our warm clothes. It felt very bulky and clumsy, and it wasn't so easy to move in them. But we had no choice; if we didn't wear them, we'd freeze.

It was a bright sunny day, and with all the snow you really needed sunglasses, which neither of us had. We certainly wouldn't need them under the ice, though. I could only hope that it was thin enough so that some of the sunlight could get through.

There were inns along the road and across a wide expanse opposite the Hardings' house. The road was only plowed as far as the Hardings', and even with snow tires with chains on them it was rough going over the snow, slipping and sliding, the wheels spinning. Sabine and I had to get out and push a couple of times. Harding tried to stay in the tracks from other vehicles. The snow was not as deep on the pier itself because it was covered with footprints that pressed it down and made it icy. We unloaded our gear onto the pier. As Harding had said, the island was only 100 yards away. I could only hope this was where the cave with my soul in it was after all. I told myself the Blue Lantern proved it.

And now came the first big moment. There was a hole in the ice just below the end of the pier. Sabine and I glanced at each other, then leaned over to see how thick the ice was.

It was a good nine inches, maybe even a foot. Since there were footprints in the snow all around it, it was clearly strong enough to walk on. We put on our tanks, and carried our flippers and the spear gun, and the underwater flashlight Sabine had brought. The one good thing was that we could walk to the island and not have to waste precious air swimming out there underwater.

Harding seemed very concerned. "You kids really sure about this, now?" he said. "I'd stay here and keep an eye out for you, but I have to go and see to the missus. At our age, you gotta take care of these injuries right away."

"Yeah, sure, we understand," I assured him. We both knew he could have helped by standing by the hole and holding on to the end of the twine, but neither of us wanted to ask him to do that instead of taking care of his wife. I felt sorry for him for not knowing what kind of thing he was married to.

We had to make two trips to the island to get all our stuff over there. We could drag stuff on the slippery ice, at least. The island was just a slab of rock with one scraggly little pine tree on it. We could see, as we approached, that there was a hole in the ice already there. When we got there we walked all the way around the island, which was about twenty feet in diameter. The only hole in the ice was on the side closest to the pier; and we needed to find the underwater cave on the "far side." Twenty feet was nothing to swim, but just because the island was twenty feet in diameter above the ice didn't mean it wasn't a lot bigger underneath—small islands, as we both knew, were just the tips of large underwater hills or mountains.

We went back and got the rest of our gear, and told Harding we didn't need the shovel and pickax, and he waved at us, looking worried, and drove slowly away. We walked back to the island. Sabine tied a big fat knot in the end of the twine and then nailed it into the ice, about a foot from the edge of the hole. Luckily, the ice was so solid it didn't crack. "I'll take the spear—I've used them before. You take the flashlight and the spool," she told me. She clipped the spool of twine onto the weight belt around my waist. It wasn't easy with the underwater mittens on, so she took them off to make sure it was as tightly fastened as possible. "And whatever happens, *don't lose this twine*. We won't be able to see the light from the hole from the other side of the island." I nodded solemnly in my tight neoprene hood. Now we couldn't put it off any longer.

The dry suits were pretty warm out here in the sun, but what was it going to be like for Sabine in the icy water? "Sabine," I said. "If you want to stand watch and wait out here, and hold on to the end of the twine, like we're supposed to, that's fine. I got myself into this. I can't get hurt until I get my soul back. But you're vulnerable. I really hate to see you risk your life because I was so stupid and—"

"You brought me here," she interrupted me gruffly. "What would be the point if I didn't go with you? And you saved my life last night. You can't carry the light and the spear gun yourself. Come on, let's get this over with."

I put on my fins and looked at the pressure gauge on the hose attached to Sabine's tank, double checking to make sure it was full. I picked up the flashlight. Then I sat down next to the hole and stuck a foot into the water.

Even with the dry suit, it was the coldest thing I'd ever felt, like putting your hand into a freezer. All my instincts were telling me to get out immediately. But I couldn't. How was Sabine, who had never been out of the tropics until now, going to deal with this? But we had no choice. I took a deep breath and with one hand on each side of the hole lowered myself in. Somehow I could sense that the water was so cold it stung, it burned. But I was impervious. It didn't bother me the way it would Sabine.

I looked up at Sabine, who was crouching over the hole, and then sank all the way under. Doing that gave me a slight feeling of freedom.

The column of light from the hole streamed down into the darkness like a spotlight, fading away at about five feet down. And it seemed as though this lake was plenty deep, maybe more than sixty-six feet, three atmospheres. I looked away from the light as Sabine dropped down, to try to let my eyes adjust to the darkness. I could just dimly make out what seemed to be rocks ahead of me—the underwater part of the island. I switched on the flashlight.

The island *was* bigger underwater. A lot bigger. And it wasn't nice and even, either, it was a massive pile of jagged rocks that vanished into the darkness in a few feet. We'd have to keep the bulk of it to our right. Finding a small cave in this thing was going to be a lot harder than I had imagined.

And above us was a thick wall of ice, blocking us off from the air, except for one small hole that would soon be far behind us.

If Sabine was bothered by the cold she wasn't showing it. She was already ahead of me in the flashlight beam. She pointed at the spool, reminding me to be careful with it. And it hit me then that we couldn't just pop up to the surface to talk whenever we felt like it. This entire maneuver was going to have to be done in complete silence, except for the constant rhythmic hiss and gurgle of the breathing gear. That was just one more part of the immensity of difficulties.

Sabine beckoned to me and started off, keeping to the right, not going down very deep. I kept turning back to look at the column of light from the hole, our only way out. The spool of twine unreeled smoothly.

Sabine was keeping out of the way of the flashlight beam, but I knew I should really be in the lead with the light. I swam ahead of her, and then around a large outcropping of rock. Now when I briefly looked back I could see no sign of the column of light from the hole, as if it didn't exist.

That was a terrible moment. I stopped swimming. *Anything* seemed better than being down here in the freezing darkness under the impenetrable roof of ice that prevented us from getting to safety. Of course, nothing could hurt me unless Sabine was right about how just holding the container of my soul might make me vulnerable. Then I'd be in as much danger as Sabine. For the time being, Sabine was the one who was risking her life—for me. She had insisted on doing this. And there was no way to get her to go back now.

I started moving forward again. This was the only way short of bank robbery to get free of Cheri Buttercup, and to stop the lethal zombie dreams. Sabine was not safe anywhere while I was a zombie. She wouldn't even be safe on St. Calao, if the plane dream was a sign of Cheri Buttercup's reach.

That was what really kept me going—wanting Sabine to be safe and for us to be together. I swam on, around another chunk of rock. I kept shining the flashlight up and down the massive bulk of the island, hoping to find the cave as soon as possible. How far had we come? Were we near the other side of the island yet? It was completely impossible to tell.

But Sabine seemed to have thought of some kind of plan, because she kept on swimming purposefully, on my left side. I went along with her, continuing to shine the flashlight up and down the island. No cave appeared.

And then, after what seemed like hours, but was really only ten minutes by my watch, the heavenly column of light came into view in the distance around a large, pointed shard of island. It blazed a bright, shimmering blue in the murky water; it was the most beautiful thing I had ever seen.

We had come a little more than halfway around. Sabine gestured and we swam back until the light was out of view for about five minutes, and then Sabine stopped. She had decided we were at the far side of the island, and she was the one with the experience. This was where the cave had to be. And we hadn't seen it yet. That meant it was not going to be easy and close to the surface. Of course not. Would Cheri Buttercup make it easy to find?

Sabine pointed down. I checked my pressure gauge. One eighth of the air was gone already. I didn't have to worry about air, but Sabine did, and looking at my gauge was a way of telling how much air she had left.

I shone the flashlight back and forth as we went down. Being deeper under the water also meant consuming air more quickly, and swimming farther out into the lake, because the island widened as it went down. The bigger the island, the harder it was going to be to find the cave.

I remembered the shark, and how I had thought being invulnerable was such a game back then. It seemed like a million years ago, in another world. And it *was* another world, in the warmth and sunshine, with constant easy access to the surface. I ached to be there now, fooling around.

And then something tugged me backward by the waist. The twine must have snagged on one of the jagged pieces of island. My heart pounding with the fear that it might break, I turned and swam back. I found it easily enough, this time, and unhooked it from the rock. But I would have to be more careful and more aware from now on. If the twine got sliced by the rock we'd really be in trouble. Yes, we had gone around the island and seen the hole, without using the twine. But it was very easy to get disoriented down here. Sabine's life depended on the security of the twine.

We continued to descend, fast, swimming back and forth beside the rock, scanning it with the flashlight beam. I checked my depth gauge. We were already forty-five feet deep—deeper than I had ever been. It was getting to the point where we would have to ascend slowly, so Sabine wouldn't get the bends.

We had to find the cave, get past any traps, find my soul, and do it all fast enough so we'd still have enough air to decompress. Without my soul I wouldn't need to decompress, but when—if—I got it back, then maybe I would. And Sabine would have to decompress no matter what.

And if we did get the bends, who would be able to take us someplace where they might be able to save our lives? Only Harding, and he was already occupied, helping his lovely wife.

I checked my air gauge. A quarter of the tank was gone. We were going to have to find the cave very soon.

Sabine grabbed my hand in its rubber mitten and pointed. She had found a big black area of emptiness in the rock. This had to be the cave. I looked at my depth gauge. We were sixty feet down, just about three atmospheres. That meant we would have to decompress for sure. We would have to go slowly to the surface, no matter what was happening, or how little air we had. And how big—or deep—the cave would be.

Sabine didn't seem fazed. She swam ahead of me now, holding the spear gun carefully with both hands, right into the empty blackness of the hole. I went after her quickly, shining the light inside.

The cave suddenly narrowed. Sabine and I had to swim close enough together to be touching each other. And then there was a blank wall in front of us. The cave turned! We were in a twisting, underwater cave, sixty feet down, under that roof of ice.

And as soon as we turned we saw something in the flashlight beam, hovering in the water, not swimming toward us or away from us, just floating there, waiting, ready to fight.

The guardian.

It was Roger.

twelve

Roger had died in a plane crash. Roger was horribly maimed and burned. I swung the flashlight away from the sight of him, trying not to gag into the breathing gear, wanting to throw up and cry at the same time.

But I couldn't avoid looking at Roger. We were going to have to see him in order to get past him. Reluctantly, I brought the beam of light back to him.

One side of his blackened face was smashed in. One of his legs was bent at an impossible angle. He was clutching a long knife in his one good hand. It was worse than anything I had ever experienced to see him floating there, staring at us. His face was too ruined to be able to read any kind of expression.

He was a *cadavre* zombie, of course—my soul had been there when they dug him up. *I* had helped make him like this.

I couldn't tell Sabine who it was. But she must know he was a zombie. No person could sustain those injuries and be alive. No person could be down in the freezing water without a tank, without a dry suit. He was invulnerable. What good would the spear gun do? I had no idea how we were going to get past him.

Roger just floated there. Those must be Cheri Buttercup's instructions. I couldn't get used to seeing him like this; it was sickening and also so heartbreaking. What could be a worse fate than to spend eternity stuck down here. Repulsive as he was, I wanted to touch him, to tell him how sorry I was. But there was nothing I could do. This was worse than when I had found out he had died.

There was a muffled *whoosh!,* and a sharply barbed spear shot toward my maimed buddy. Part of me wanted to stop her from shooting at him—I knew she couln't hurt him, and this was Roger, my best friend.

Despite how ruined his body was, in the water Roger moved effortlessly out of the way, and the spear sank down uselessly below. Sabine quickly pulled it back and fitted it into the gun.

When he moved to the side we could see that he was chained to the rock. It was a long chain. But why did he have to be chained at all, if he was a zombie under her control? Did that mean he wasn't *completely* under her control?

I kept expecting him to attack Sabine, the vulnerable one. But he didn't. He just floated there, his ruined mouth half open, teeth sticking out at all angles, his blackened eyes unblinking in the flashlight beam, staring at us, clutching his long, sharp knife. What was he waiting for? Why wasn't he doing something?

And then I understood Cheri Buttercup's strategy. The longer he made us wait, the sooner Sabine's air would run out. She'd have to swim away and get to the hole, ascending too fast, and get the bends and die. Or else she'd get hypothermia from being in this freezing water for so long, and die from that.

Unless Sabine got out of the water soon and left me alone with this Roger thing. But Sabine seemed to have no intention of deserting me. I would pay her back for this, I would do anything to pay her back. If we ever got out of here.

And Sabine wasn't wasting any time. Poor Roger was right there in easy range. Sabine fired the spear again, taking a little more time to aim this time, since now she knew the thing was just sitting there, not darting around trying to get away from her.

This time Roger didn't even bother moving out of its path. The sharp spear hit him in what was left of his face and bounced right off. Sabine reeled it back again. What good did she think it was now?

She tugged at my arm and began slowly moving deeper into the cave. If Roger wasn't going to attack, maybe we could swim past him to the bottle where my soul was.

The closer I got to him the more I wanted to reach out to him, to apologize somehow for being the reason he was in this hell. But there was nothing I could do. I could hardly bear it.

And then suddenly, unexpectedly, because he had done nothing for so long, Roger darted toward me with incredible speed. But that was crazy! He was put there by Cheri Buttercup. He knew he couldn't hurt me.

He didn't try. He simply sliced off the twine on my waist with his knife, the twine that was attached to the hole in the ice, our only means of escape. It swept away too quickly for me to grab it.

I wanted to give up then and there and head back for where we remembered the hole might be. But not Sabine.

As soon as Roger had cut the twine he went back to where he had been, floating near the cave wall. I kept the light focused on him, still fighting tears. I could feel Sabine in the water beside me. She seemed to be taking more careful aim with the spear gun than ever. I didn't understand.

The spear shot forward again. It went through a link in the chain close to Roger and then rammed into a crack in the wall behind him. Now he was pinned to the wall. He immediately began trying to pull the spear out of the crack, but it seemed to be really wedged in there, and with only one good hand, already holding the knife, he wasn't strong enough to get it out.

Why had Cheri Buttercup picked this maimed thing to be the guardian, instead of something stronger? Only to torment me.

Roger was stuck now. We could get into the cave. I felt like hugging Sabine. But more than half the air in my tank was gone. That meant that Sabine's was more than half empty, too. And once we found my soul, however hard that was going to be, it was going to take us much longer than we expected to find our way back to the escape hole, now that we didn't have the twine to guide us.

Sabine dropped the spear gun—we didn't need it now. She beckoned impatiently. I shone the flashlight around the back of the cave, hoping the bottle with my soul in it would not be too hard to find. Time was really running out now.

The bottle wasn't hard to find. There it was. And there another one was. And another, and another. The entire back wall of the cave was piled with perfume bottles. Perfume bottles! So like Cheri Buttercup! And which one held my soul?

You would have thought I would be able to sense which one it was, just because it held my own soul. But for some reason— probably something Cheri Buttercup had worked into the spell—I had no sense of it at all. We were going to have to go through them, and see if I would know it when I held the bottle. And there were dozens of them.

I shook my arms and lifted my hands at Sabine in a kind of

shrug. Clearly she understood, because instantly we were both attacking the bottles, me feeling as many as I could, Sabine passing more to me.

I checked my air gauge. It was a quarter full. Sabine was going to have to get out of here soon; she would need time to decompress. I started gesturing at her to go.

She shook her head adamantly and pointed at me. And then I understood. Sure, nothing could hurt me now. I could stay underwater even without air. I didn't have to worry about decompressing. Now.

But as soon as I got the bottle with my soul in it, I might die if I had no air. The faster we got through the bottles the more chance we'd have. How could I ever, ever, ever pay her back?

And what did it mean about the way she felt for me?

I worked faster, constantly checking my air gauge. Now there was only an eighth of a tank left. Sabine was going to have to get out of here. I would have to get my soul back on my own. And if I didn't, Sabine would never be safe from me again. It just seemed too unfair to be possible!

If I couldn't find my soul I'd have tell my parents everything and only hope they'd believe—unlikely as that was—and come up with fifty thousand dollars. I'd have to keep fighting off the dreams until they did. Though I would prefer to kill Cheri Buttercup than give her all that money and let her have the last laugh. Rage filled me.

But rage wasn't going to help me now. I picked up another bottle, a Calvin Klein one.

And I knew. This was the one with my soul in it. I could feel it tingle in my hands as soon as I touched the bottle. None of the others had done that.

I grabbed Sabine's hand and pointed at the bottle, making it clear that this was the right one. Without thinking, I started to open it.

She slapped my hand to stop me. Then I remembered again what she had said about not opening it. I didn't understand, but Sabine knew about these things and she had been right about everything so far.

I clutched the bottle with my soul in it. We were out of the cave in a flash, zooming past sad, ruined Roger, still helplessly struggling to pull the spear out of the crack in the wall. Glad as I was to get my soul back, it hurt to see him. If only we could set him free! But there was no time. And as a *cadavre* zombie, there was no way to free him from Cheri Buttercup.

And then I knew what the chain was for. It was to trap *me* in the cave of souls, with dead Roger, forever. That's why he was struggling so frantically. But because of the way the spear had lodged itself into the chain and the wall, *he* was trapped. It didn't bear thinking about.

Outside the cave Sabine carefully pointed at herself and then at me, indicating I should do exactly what she did. She only had a few minutes of air left and we had to ascend slowly, starting now, not waiting until we found the hole but decompressing on the way there—if we ever did find it in time.

I could see that Sabine was weakening from the cold—her strokes did not have the force they usually did. And now that we were swimming hard again I felt the weakness, too, which I hadn't felt before. I hadn't let my soul out of the bottle, but I had it with me now. Did that mean I was vulnerable again, or not? Would we be strong enough to get as far as the hole, even if we were lucky enough to find it?

Sabine was leading me around the rocks to the left, gradually ascending, almost a foot with each stroke of her arms. I did my best to keep the light focused just ahead of her, while cradling the bottle under my other arm.

But where was the hole? It hadn't seemed this far before. We kept swimming, going slower and slower from cold and weakness.

Sabine checked her pressure gauge and twisted the emergency valve that gave her five more minutes of air. I did too, just in case.

The water was as dark and murky as ever. If I died, there was a reason for it: I had been a stupid jerk to make that deal in the first place. But Sabine dying because of my stupidity was unthinkable. And we were so close to making it back. We kept swimming and swimming and not seeing the hole. Minutes ticked by. *Where was the hole? Where was the—*

And then, around a rock, the shining blue column appeared. It was the most gloriously beautiful thing I had ever seen in my life. It *was* Sabine's life. And it was not as far above us as it had been the last time we'd seen it. Sabine was smart all right.

And then I tried to take a breath and no air came out. The tank was empty. What was Sabine going to do?

Sabine's must have gone empty at the same moment. She turned back to me and gestured frantically. Then she took the breathing tube out of her mouth, and I could see bubbles of air coming out of her lips. Why was she blowing out the last air she had?

So she wouldn't get the bends. The air inside her might still be compressed, even though we had ascended slowly. The less air in her lungs when she reached the surface, the safer she would be.

Blowing air *out* of my lungs in this situation was so counterintuitive that it was almost impossible. But Sabine was the expert. I took out the breathing gear and blew air out slowly as I swam.

Sabine expelled a last breath of air and pulled herself up out of the hole, flapping her fins. She got her legs out quickly to make room for me. I stuck my head out of the water and met her eyes before taking my first gasp of natural air. She looked exhausted, but she was not curled up in agony. I breathed in the cold outside air.

And Sabine was safe from me now. I had my soul back! Even though I hadn't opened the bottle, I could sense that the hollowness I had felt about everything except Sabine was gone. I was free of Cheri Buttercup. We had beaten her at her own game, and won, without paying her fifty thousand dollars.

We hugged each other for a long time, not speaking, just catching our breath. Then we began dragging our gear back. Without the spear gun we could carry all of it in one trip.

"That . . . that was my friend Roger down there, guarding the cave," I told her. "The one who died in the plane crash. He was the reason I went to see Cheri Buttercup. She asked me his name the first time I saw her. And one of my first dreams was about digging him up and bringing him back to life. She put him there to wait for me. And to trap me there forever." I still wished we could have set him free.

"She's a monster," Sabine muttered bitterly. "Don't you dare open that bottle until I tell you to. If you keep it in the bottle, she'll think you got trapped in the cave by Roger and never got out. Or that you never found it. That could make a big difference in the end. And you *have* gotten it back now, whether it's open or not, even though she doesn't know it."

Okay, it was great to have my soul back. But I still couldn't stop thinking about Roger being trapped down there.

"And in the summer," Sabine said harshly, "we have to come back here and smash all the other bottles. And do something about Roger. We have to save up the money and do it, no matter what. *Nothing* is more important than freeing all her zombies, and destroying her power."

Her anger startled my thoughts away from Roger and the soul in my hand.

"Sabine?" I said. "Are you okay?"

"Come on," she said. "I'm freezing."

I looked back at the hole. I had to remind myself that Roger could feel nothing now, that he didn't really know we were leaving him in another grave. I turned away. We'd come back in the summer, just as Sabine had said. Or sooner.

A couple of guys were fishing on the pier, and of course they had a million questions, and we did our best to fend them off. They did give us a ride back to the house, so we didn't have to walk the whole way. Even though we had accomplished what we had set out to do, we wanted to get back to New York as soon as possible—the sooner I got back, the less trouble I would be in. And I had so little money left. How much was Harding going to charge us?

Harding's car was outside the house. He must have taken his wife to the doctor and back already. We hoped he would be able to give us a lift to the bus stop.

When he opened the door for us he looked very happy and relieved. Ice was already forming on our dry suits. "Into the hot shower, ladies first," he said. "Hope you won't be going out into the water again."

"No way," I said. "But we're kind of in a hurry. We need to catch the next bus to Syracuse as soon as possible."

He threw back his head and laughed. "Boy, the only bus out of here to *anywhere* leaves at 8:00 A.M. this time of year. Anyway, you need rest and comfort and you're welcome here for another night, no problem.

We looked at each other and we were both thinking the same thing: Mrs. Harding.

"Oh, we couldn't impose on you any more than we already have," I said. "You haven't even told us how much money we owe you. If you could just give us a lift to a motel, then we wouldn't be a bother to you anymore. Especially with your wife hurting her foot. We wouldn't want her to have to do any work, cooking for us or anything."

He laughed, shaking his head. "Oh, the missus is fine. Doc's got her in a little bandage thingy and she's as good as new. Anyway, there just *ain't* no motels open here at this time of year. Not a one. No way I'm letting you out of this house until tomorrow morning. And whatever I might ask you to pay, I'm sure you can afford it. No need to worry about the money. No need at all."

thirteen

Mrs. Harding was as quiet and sweet as ever, not hobbling at all in her rubberlike ankle brace and big fluffy bunny slippers. After we had both had hot showers and put on our warmest clothes, she served us hot tomato soup and toasted cheese sandwiches and cocoa. It hit the spot. It was great to feel hungry again.

Alone in my room, I studied the bottle with my soul in it. I could feel my soul had come back to me, in a way, but there was still a blue wisp of something remaining in the bottle. Now I understood why Sabine insisted that we not open it. So I wrapped up the bottle very carefully in a thick T-shirt, and put it in my backpack, with a lot of soft things around it. I didn't want anything to happen to it.

We knew we should really be getting out of here, but the

difficulties seemed insurmountable, unless we wanted to stand by the roadside hitchhiking with all our gear in the cold. And after this morning our bodies just didn't want to do that. Something was lulling us into spending the afternoon under blankets on the couches, in the warm, quiet house, with books and magazines.

And each other. I had not met Sabine until after my soul had been taken from me by Cheri Buttercup. Even then, in that odd, cold state, I had felt what I thought was a very strong affection for her.

It was a shadow of what I felt for her now. And that feeling was only intensified by what she had done for me under the lake, the terrible risk she had taken to save me from my own mistake.

I found myself forgetting my book and just looking at her, my heart swelling so deeply it hurt.

The fact that I felt so different had to mean I had my soul back, at least partially, even though I had not let it out of the bottle. I would have to take very good care of that bottle.

I didn't know how to tell Sabine about this feeling for her, I didn't have the words. But I didn't have to. Because she would see me looking at her that way, and our eyes would meet, and we didn't need to say anything. I know it sounds cornball, but I can't help it. It felt terrible and wonderful.

Except for the fact that she had to go back to St. Calao in only a few days. That tore me up a lot. I wished I didn't have to think about missing her.

And there was also the little matter of having to spend another night in the same house with Mrs. Harding. She might be just as violent as before. On the other hand, if Sabine was right, Cheri Buttercup didn't *know* I had my soul back. She would have expected me to get trapped, or never find it, rather than accomplish this nearly impossible task. So we might be safe from attack. And we might not.

We tried to plan some kind of strategy to protect ourselves. It was difficult, because we couldn't predict what Mrs. Harding would do. Sabine had been the target before, because Cheri Buttercup must have realized that if anybody could make it possible for me to get my soul back, it was Sabine. It was clearer than ever that Cheri Buttercup knew somebody on the island. Sabine said it bothered her, wondering who it could be. But it didn't seem to bother her as much as her need to free Cheri Buttercup's zombies. As close as I felt to her, as grateful as I was for what she had done, Sabine puzzled me more than ever now.

But we had to think about practical things. The other problem about Mrs. Harding was that last night I had been invulnerable. But now I might be normal again. Cheri Buttercup probably didn't know it. But could Mrs. Harding tell? Did that mean Mrs. Harding would be after me, too?

But if she really wanted to get to me, the best way to do it would be to kill Sabine. The more we thought about it, the more we guessed that Sabine would be the target again. If only Mr. Harding wasn't such a stickler for propriety, I could have stayed in Sabine's room overnight, to help her defend herself! But maybe there were ways we could get around that limitation.

Dinner was a roast chicken, with delicious stuffing and mashed potatoes and gravy. Whatever else she was, Mrs. Harding sure was a good cook. I would have enjoyed the meal more if I weren't worrying about what she would do tonight—and also about money. Mr. Harding still refused to talk about how much we owed him. He probably wouldn't accept a credit card, and I had only ninety dollars cash—and no return bus ticket.

After supper Sabine and I had another conference in her room, four feet on the floor. "You know, I was thinking," I said. "I assumed Mr. Harding didn't know about his wife. But—she *must* have attacked other people. Obviously she was like this before we came along, and for a reason, too. So don't you think he would have noticed the other attacks? There must have been some repercussions."

"It's easy for people not to see things they don't want to see, believe me," Sabine said.

"Something like your wife trying to kill somebody in the same house?" I said. "Seems kind of hard to ignore something like that. And it makes me think something I don't want to think."

"Now what?" She seemed a little afraid of what I was going to say.

"The only reason he wouldn't notice, and not do anything about it, is if he's one, too."

"Then where was he last night?"

"Maybe they didn't think he was necessary, because she and I were already there. And that it would be better if you and I didn't know about him—we'd trust him then and not be so careful. I don't know what they think about me anymore. She didn't seem surprised that I was one, and yet I had no way of telling anything about her, until it happened. But the main point is, the attack last night didn't work. Tonight's could be worse. I think we should both try to stay awake all night. We don't need to do anything tomorrow except sleep on the bus. If he'll even take us to the bus stop. And if we can even get a ticket."

Mr. Harding shooed me off to my room again. It had been a long, hard morning, but we had both rested a lot in the afternoon, and we were both nervous and alert. The minutes and the hours ticked away as I sat on my bed in the dark room. I wore one of Cheri Buttercup's pantyhose on my arm and Sabine wore the other. We didn't know if they would have any power now that I was no longer a zombie, but anything was worth a try.

I sat up with a start. I had dozed off. It was after 4:00 A.M. The house was absolutely quiet. Had they gone after Sabine, had they gotten her, without touching me? It was just the kind of thing Cheri Buttercup would do, if she knew—take away the most important person to me in the world. I didn't care about Mr. Harding's little rules now.

I got the underwater flashlight and moved quietly out into the empty hallway. Sabine's door was shut. I was so scared my heart seemed to me to be the loudest thing in the house. I gritted my teeth and then knocked. "Sabine, it's me," I said. "Are you awake? Are you okay?"

There was no answer.

If they had done anything to her I would get them for it, I would spend my life getting them and Cheri Buttercup, I swore it. Sabine had not locked the door—we didn't think it would matter because Mrs. Harding could get through it anyway, and we wanted me to have access to the room. I pushed the door open, dreading what I was about to see, and turned on the flashlight.

Sabine was lying in bed breathing peacefully, huddled under a pile of blankets. It *did* seem colder than usual in the house. I went quietly closer. "Sabine," I whispered.

She sat up abruptly. "Oh, no, I fell asleep," she whispered. "What's going on?"

"Nothing. And it's four in the morning already. You'd think they would have struck by now."

"Yeah, you would," she agreed. "And why is it so cold?"

"So . . . do we look around, check the place out? Do we just keep waiting? What do you think?"

"Well, if we just stay here in this room with no exit, we're at a big disadvantage. No reason not to look around. Easier to run that way, if we have to."

Neither of us had gotten undressed for bed—that had been part of the plan, so we'd be alert and ready. But it was still oddly cold, so we both wrapped blankets around ourselves. First we checked the upstairs. Nobody there but us. We crept down the stairway, which luckily was carpeted and did not creak. Mr. and Mrs. Harding's bedroom was right at the bottom of the stairs. The door was wide open. We gave each other an odd look, then peeked inside.

There was nobody there. The bed was unmade, just a bare mattress with no sheets or blankets or pillowcases. It didn't look like it had been slept in for months. We were both too mystified to say anything.

I gestured to her to come and look around more of the unheated house. The curtains were all closed, the shades drawn. Dust cloths covered the furniture in the living room. But strangest of all was the kitchen. Everything was packed up, as if in storage. The refrigerator was completely empty, no leftover chicken, no milk, nothing. And the refrigerator wasn't cold at all, no ice or frost in the freezer, no hum.

That gave me an idea. I went around flipping light switches. Not one of them worked. No electricity. I turned on the kitchen faucet. No water came out.

I shook my head at Sabine, so disoriented I seriously wondered if I was going crazy. "If I didn't know any better, I'd say the place was closed up for the winter. It looks like nobody's been here for months."

"They did all this since we went to our rooms at ten o'clock?" Sabine said. "Is that possible? Wouldn't we have heard them moving stuff around?"

"Yes, we would have. I was listening." I felt chills now, and it wasn't just because of the unheated house. But Sabine was seeing it, too; maybe I wasn't crazy.

"Ken," Sabine said, "it's like—they weren't here. They were never really here. Not as people, anyway. You were right about him, too. They stayed in Syracuse all winter, like they said they were going to do from now on."

"What are you talking about? We just said good night to them a few hours ago. Are you nuts?"

"Listen, Ken. Cheri Buttercup must have known we were going to make the dive today—that's why she made you and Mrs. Harding attack me last night. Now your soul is still in the bottle. It was never released. So she *does* think you're trapped in the underwater cave—that's the most likely thing, anyway. So she doesn't need her astral zombies here. It's like . . . the whole *house* is astral, too."

"Huh?" I said.

"Come on," Sabine said. She raced to the front of the house, pulled open the shade, and looked out the window. There was no car, and the road was heavily drifted with snow. It had not been plowed.

My mouth dropped open. "But . . ." I said. "But this is . . . it's not possible."

"Astral zombies are real," Sabine said. "Their master can whisk them away in a second. Remember when you attacked me on the plane? And since she believes your body is trapped in the cave, she doesn't need the Hardings here anymore. We were probably the only people who even saw them." She gestured around her. "Everything we saw was astral. And now it's gone. This *proves* she thinks your body is trapped, and can't do anything, and that she has your soul for good."

Then Sabine got immediately practical. "We're going to have to hitchhike to the bus stop, with all the company's gear." She looked at her watch. It was almost five o'clock now. "We better start getting ready. It's going to be a long walk if we don't get a lift. And the tanks are heavy. We can't risk missing that bus. If we get there early we can wait inside the market."

It didn't take us long to pack because we hadn't brought much, and most of what we brought we were wearing. A cup of something hot would have been nice, but we couldn't even heat water on the electric stove. We were hungry, too, but there was no food at all in the house. We went out the same unlocked window Sabine had used to get back inside when she jumped out last night. Luckily I had a good pair of boots and had bought an adequate pair for Sabine. It wasn't easy getting through the drifts to the main road wearing the heavy tanks on our backs and carrying the other gear. And it was quite dark, without any stars. It was a good thing we still had the underwater flashlight. As we plowed our way through the drifts, it began to snow.

"Great," I muttered. "Getting down out of the mountains in a snowstorm."

"You're lucky to be alive at all—we both are," Sabine reminded me. I couldn't argue with her.

It was still dark when we reached the main road, but the going was a lot easier here. We trudged slowly along, bowed down by the tanks. There were hardly any cars, and none of them so much as slowed when I stuck my thumb out.

"That Cheri Buttercup person is really powerful," Sabine said. "And she's going to be furious about losing you—*and* fifty thousand dollars—if she ever finds out. You better be really, really careful now. Watch out for everything. That's the other reason not to let your soul out of the bottle until she's taken care of."

I knew she was right, and I was scared. Cheri Buttercup cared a lot about money and power, and those people are dangerous. But I didn't want to think about it at this exact moment. I shifted the tank on my back. "I just wish Harding had left his car, with a set of keys in it."

We decided it would be better if Sabine was the one who stood in front when a car came by, so they'd be sure to see it was a girl and not two guys. And finally an old pickup stopped for us. It didn't have an extra cab, so we had to all squeeze into the front seat, with no seat belts. The driver was a young guy with long hair and a beard who didn't talk much. Neither did we. I liked thrill rides, but, like Harding, this guy was going faster than I would have on this road—and it was slipperier now because of the snow, which was getting heavier. Luckily it was not a long ride.

And the market was open, and they let us wait inside in the warmth. They even had a small deli section with sandwiches and hot tea. But I only had ninety dollars and we had to somehow pay for the bus. We were getting hungrier and hungrier.

The bus came rumbling slowly along, its headlights on in the dim light. We waved and waved. The driver looked at us balefully when he came down to open the storage compartment under the bus. "I wasn't even gonna do the route today if there was nobody in Dunwich," he said. He looked at the sky, shading his eyes. "The mountain's gonna be real bad." He scratched his head. "In fact, maybe you two better just go back where you were staying and wait until tomorrow when it won't be so—"

"Oh, please, you have to take us to Syracuse," Sabine said in her sweetest voice. "It's so important for us to get back as soon as possible. My mother's sick in the hospital and everything. They just called to tell us."

He sighed. But he got back into the bus. There was nobody else on it. "Tickets, please," he said.

"Er . . . I was hoping I could put it on a credit card. I don't have a hundred and eight dollars in cash," I said.

"No way," he said. "It's the rules. Only cash on the bus, and it goes into this box I can't open."

I was desperate to get out of here. We had no place to stay! "How about if I just paid for the ride from here to Syracuse? I'll buy the ticket to New York at the Syracuse station."

"Thirty-five bucks each," he said. "And there's an ATM at the station in Syracuse, if that's any help," he added more kindly.

The ATM was no help, because I had no money in my account. I gave him $70, feeling desperate. I had only $20 left. How were we going to get back home? How were we going to get anything to eat? We were hungrier than ever now.

And only then did it hit me. We had done it, I had my soul back. It didn't matter if my parents and the cops traced us now. I could use the credit card from now on. It was a huge feeling of relief.

The relief didn't last very long. We sat in front, but we could hardly see a thing, the snow was falling so thick and fast. And even though we were crawling along, we still kept skidding on the downhill curves. Skidding in a bus is a lot scarier than skidding in a car—a bus is much longer and the skid goes on for a longer time, sliding to the side more. "Can zombie masters control the weather?" I asked Sabine.

She rolled her eyes. "No. We're in enough trouble without you letting your imagination run away with you. *Bokors* can't control the weather. There are limits to everything," she said. "But one thing I do know for sure. And I'm going to keep reminding you. That lady you made the deal with is going to be mad, real mad, when she finds out you got your soul back. She has to be. And she'll want the money and she's not going to leave you alone until she gets it. And I won't be here to hold your hand. You're going to be on your own."

Tough and outspoken as she was, I loved her. I squeezed her hand. I could feel that she was as uncomfortable on this road in this weather as I was—maybe even more so, because she was so unfamiliar with weather like this. Holding hands helped us both.

There was wind now, too, battering at the bus. It felt like it might even push us off the road. I could see the driver fighting the wind with the steering wheel. And the wind made the skidding worse.

And then, suddenly, a jackknifed truck loomed out of nowhere, stuck at right angles to the road. Sabine and I both screamed. Our driver violently swung the wheel and just barely managed to get the bus around the rear of the truck, grazing it only slightly, and skidding worse than ever. We kept skidding for what seemed like forever, until he got it back under control.

I looked over at him right after that. The bus wasn't real warm, but sweat was dripping down his temples. He was a brave guy.

It was bliss when we finally pulled up at the station in Syracuse. It had taken two hours to get from Syracuse to Dunwich, going uphill. The trip down in the blizzard had taken four. Knowing I could use the credit card now, I tried to give the bus driver my last $20, but he wouldn't take it.

It was noon. Oddly, the bus station was full. Piles of bags were everywhere, all the seats were occupied, and people were sitting on the floor. Not what I had expected. I waited on a long ticket window line, which snaked around. Just a few days ago, I would have cut. Not now. Anyway, these people didn't look like they'd let me get away with it, not even the old ladies.

"A lot of buses cancelled to New York today," the ticket man said, half an hour later, and I was sure he enjoyed telling me this after I had waited for so long. "The best you're going to do is the overnight bus at midnight—*if* the weather clears. Luckily there's two seats. Not together."

I charged the tickets. Now we had over eleven hours to kill at the Syracuse bus station in a blizzard. This was not the kind of thing that you usually imagined happened on adventures.

We were starving. I tried to buy food with the credit card, realizing that I would need my cash to get a taxi from Port Authority bus station in New York. But the little sandwich place did not take credit cards. It had cost $12 to take a cab from the hotel to Port Authority, so it would be about $15 to get from there to my house. I bought the cheapest sandwich, turkey with nothing, for $5, and we split it. It was so small it hardly made any difference.

So it was boring, and we were starving, and there's not much to say about it. But we were together. We appreciated every minute we had left before Sabine had to fly home.

I built up the nerve to call my parents, putting it on the card.

Mom picked it up in the middle of the first ring. "Hello? Hello?" she said.

"Hi, Mom," I said.

"Oh, Ken, Ken! Are you okay? She's letting you call?"

"What? Who's letting me call?"

"That awful woman who said she'd bring you back for a hundred thousand dollars."

"*What?*" I screamed into the phone. "You didn't pay her anything, did you?"

"No, no, she said we could wait another day before you died. We told the police, even though she told us not to. They couldn't trace her or you. But I don't understand. You got away from her?"

"No, no. She never had me. She's lying. Don't do anything until we get there. We're in the Syracuse bus station and we'll be back early tomorrow morning. Then we'll explain everything."

"What do you mean, 'we'?"

There was no point in lying about it. "Me and Sabine, the girl from St. Calao."

"That girl? What's *she* doing here?"

"I'll tell you, I'll tell you. We're getting back to New York on the bus early tomorrow morning. We'll take a cab from Port Authority. It'll be too early for much traffic."

"Oh, thank God you're okay. Thank . . . God you're okay." She was sobbing now.

"Mom! Stop! What's the weather like there? If the weather's bad the bus isn't going to go."

She gasped, trying to control herself, "Just flurries here, I don't think they expect more than that. Let me know as soon as you find out if the bus is going to go or not. Oh, Ken, I could kill you for getting into this mess, whatever it is, but I love you. We've both been . . . sick."

"I'll let you know about the bus. We'll be back sometime tomorrow. Then I'll explain everything. I . . . love you." It wasn't easy to say that, but it got her off the phone.

Sabine was as thrilled as I was to hear about Cheri Buttercup's attempt at extorting money from my parents. It was a big, greedy blunder on her part, and it might give me an edge. It also meant for sure she didn't know I had the bottle with my soul in it. She really did think she had trapped me in the cave of souls. And she was *still* trying to get money out of my parents.

The bus did go on time, and Sabine got the man next to her to change seats with me so we could sit together, curled up on the seat and whispering about what we could do to make sure Cheri Buttercup would never be able to get at me.

The next day, Friday, we got a cab back to our apartment. I had one dollar left.

And after I dealt with Mom and Dad, we would start working on Cheri Buttercup.

fourteen

Mom and Dad were furious and relieved at the same time, and they both hugged me. And when I told them Sabine had saved my life—that I'd be dead for sure if I hadn't brought her from St. Calao—they hugged her, too.

Then they wanted to know everything.

I said we had to have food. While we shoveled down scrambled eggs and bacon and toast, I just told them the truth, about Cheri Buttercup killing me, and taking my soul, and making me a zombie. I didn't know what else to do. I was in no state of mind to come up with some lie that would make sense to them and make sense to the police and make Mom and Dad not mad at me. I was careful to leave out any reference to Cheri Buttercup's real name or where she lived. If the cops found that out they'd just go and get her before we carried out our scheme, and we both knew that would never work, not with her.

They kept stopping me to ask questions and express their disbelief. And of course in the end they attributed the whole thing to this woman being a charlatan and trying to get me killed by convincing me I had to dive under the ice or pay her $50,000. They were surprised I was so naïve and gullible, and said they would be eternally grateful to Sabine for helping me—though they were mad at her, too, for going along with such dangerous foolishness.

They did believe we had really dived under the ice, though. We couldn't have described what it had been like if we hadn't. The part about the ice made them more furious at Cheri Buttercup than I had ever seen them. I was glad of that for several reasons. One of them was that it deflected a lot of their anger away from me.

Then they called the cops on the case, who came and questioned me, too. Again, I was especially careful not to tell them where Cheri Buttercup lived or what her name was, though they kept trying to get it out of me.

It was Friday, and Sabine's flight wasn't until Sunday. Sabine wanted to be here to help me beat Cheri Buttercup.

"You're going to have to tell us her name sometime, and where she lives," the head cop told me for the tenth time. The two cops glanced at each other, and nodded, and then the head cop said, "There've been some other cases like this, people saying some woman had control over them, making them commit crimes. But they all disappeared before we could find out any information about her—they were afraid to tell. Now you're here, and you know who she is. What she did to a kid your age is criminally insane; it's close to murder. And on top of it, trying to extort all that money from your parents." He shook his head. "People like that shouldn't be allowed to . . . to practice, or whatever they call it. They should be locked up. And now we have someone who knows who she is, and still won't tell."

"Okay, she may be insane, but she's smart—really smart," I said. "If you want to get her, we're going to have to be really, really careful about it. She'll slip out of your hands otherwise. Whatever you may believe about her powers—or her lack of powers—she can get away with a lot of things. Can we make a deal and do it our way?"

"We're the experts," the cop said, of course.

"Did you ever elude the police for three days and scuba dive in a cave under the ice and come out of it alive?" I asked him.

"Well, no," he said. "But I don't see what that has to do with criminally charging this woman."

"It shows we know what we're doing," I told him. "Do you remember what I said about the people whose house we stayed in disappearing, like they'd never been there? And the plowed road getting unplowed, before it started to snow again?"

"Pretty hard to believe that, kid."

"Did you see it, Sabine?" I asked her.

"I saw it," Sabine said. "It happened. I've lived in the Caribbean all my life. Zombies are real. Astral zombies, *cadavre* zombies. I can give you the exact recipe she uses to make people into zombies, if you want." There was something very convincing about the way she said it—she could do that.

"This woman makes things like that happen. We're going to have to be very careful to catch her," I said.

The cop sighed. "So what do you have in mind?"

At least we had gotten him to agree to listen to our plan without giving them the information about her.

"First of all, we can't let her know I'm back. She has ways of finding out things, so we have to prove to her that I'm not back yet and that Mom and Dad are desperate enough to pay her that money to get me back."

"*What?*" Dad said. "You want me to give her a hundred thousand dollars for no reason? What new craziness are you going to come up with next?"

"Because we have to have proof. If we just go and accuse her, she'll deny everything and say I'm crazy. And who will a jury believe? Her, or two teenagers with a nutty zombie story? And how can you prove she was the one who called you and asked for all that money? Of course I don't want you to *really* give her the money. We just have to tempt her and get her to reveal herself. Is there any other way to prove it?"

Nobody said anything. They didn't have an argument. Even though they weren't ready to admit it yet, they had to know I was right.

"How were you supposed to contact her?" I asked them.

"We were supposed to call her at a public phone booth number today at noon. She said if we told the police the number the deal was off and we'd never see you again." Mom started crying as she said it. "How could anybody be so cruel? Taking advantage of . . . of . . ."

"Excuse me," Sabine said, with a steely edge to her voice. "But that's exactly why we have to be careful and really get her. So she won't go on doing these things to other people. And Ken won't be safe either until she's locked up."

"So at noon you have to call her and make an arrangement to drop off the cash and pick me up," I said. "It doesn't have to be real money, it can be a suitcase full of paper." And then we told them the rest of the plan.

None of them liked it. They thought it was too dangerous. But all the alternatives they came up with had whopping holes. Sabine and I had spent a lot of time on this. We knew I'd only be safe if Cheri Buttercup was stopped for good. And this was the only way we could get her to dig her own grave.

Dad called her at noon. I didn't dare to listen on the extension for fear she might hear me breathing, and anyway the head cop wanted to hear.

"Hello. This is George Pritchard," Dad said, sounding very serious. "We're desperate. What do you want us to do?"

There was a pause. "Yeah?" He wrote down instructions on a pad of paper. "Yes, yes, for sure. No cops, plainclothes or otherwise, no nothing. We don't want to take any risks. This is too important. We just want our son back." He made a few more notes. "He'll be there for sure?" he said. "Because if he's not, you won't get a penny, and we'll hunt you down till your dying day." He hung up.

"So what does she want?" I asked him impatiently. She was really vile. She didn't have me and she was still trying to get all that money from Dad. Again, I fought to control my rage against her. I was beginning to get pretty good at it.

"Well, she already gave me all this real information to prove she knows a lot about you. She wants me to leave the money in a briefcase in a phone booth in Queens. She insists you'll be there. How is that possible? And what makes her think I'm going to leave the money when you're not there?"

Sabine and I looked at each other. I knew we were thinking the same thing. Cheri Buttercup thought she still had control of my soul. And at least part of my soul was still trapped in the bottle, possibly still under her control, possibly still dangerous.

"I hope this plan of yours is going to work," Dad said. "I would have expected a locker at Penn Station or something."

"Too tricky, getting her the key and everything," the head cop said. "And security is always suspicious of bags sitting alone in transportation areas. Phone booths are popular for this kind of thing. Especially now when so many people have cell phones and don't use the booths as much."

We were pretty sure she'd be hiding behind a bush so that she could whisk the briefcase out of the phone booth the second Dad was out of sight—she wouldn't want to leave the money sitting there for any length of time. We were also sure she'd pick up the money herself—money was so important to her that she wouldn't trust anybody else to do it, not even a zombie slave. She must have learned that she could not always trust zombie slaves, because she had never gotten me to hurt Sabine. The police kept saying they wanted to station some plainclothes cops in the area, but we argued and argued with them. We were afraid she'd be suspicious.

The biggest risk was that she might catch sight of me. We could only hope that she wouldn't be on the lookout, since if I were around why would Dad be going through with this?

I had only met Cheri Buttercup twice, and Sabine had never met her at all. So we didn't know much about her personality, except that she was greedy, and totally without regard for anyone in the world except herself. We couldn't be sure she would do what we hoped she would do. The surprise element was what we had going for us. We promised the cops that if our plan didn't work, we would then tell them all the information about her.

We were also pretty sure they were lying to us about the plainclothes cops. Before they left the house I said, "Look, if you insist on having any plainclothes cops in the area, have them really far away. If she notices any tricks she won't show, and then she'll make sure you never find her again. I don't know how, but she will. So please, keep them really, really far away. You want to get her, right?"

"Right," the cop said expressionlessly. He clearly didn't like taking orders from a sixteen-year-old.

After the cops left, Mom and Dad outlined their plans for grounding me indefinitely. Home right after school every day; no after-school clubs or sports; no dates, even on weekends; half my previous allowance. I tried not to yawn. None of it mattered at all. Sabine wouldn't be around, so I didn't care who I saw or what I did. Anyway, most of my friends had already deserted me, the last time I thought about it. And as for Kaitlin, Adams could have her. I didn't even want to have to see her in homeroom.

Dad gave us an old briefcase and we cut up a lot of newspapers and old magazines. I put all new batteries in my pocket micro-casette tape recorder. I cleaned the lenses on the good pair of binoculars, and made sure the digital camera was working.

When Sabine and I were alone I said, without much hope, "Maybe my parents could send you to school here, in New York. Then you'd get an education, you could do something with your life, you wouldn't be stuck being a scuba instructor forever. And we . . . could be together."

She shook her head. "I can't leave my father. He can't really take care of himself—it was hard enough finding people to step in for me for this one week. I want to be together, too, but . . ." She shrugged, not meeting my eye. "I just don't see how it's possible."

She always used her father as an excuse, and yet she had never let me meet him.

"I'll figure something out. I will, I will," I said.

Nervous as we were about the next day, we hadn't slept much on the bus and had been up for a long time. We slept well that night, and woke up early on Saturday morning, ready to go with my father to Queens.

fifteen

The weather was beautiful on Saturday, sunny, and the warmest day we'd had yet. This was inconvenient for us, because it was almost too warm to wear jackets with hoods, and I had to have a hood so I wouldn't be recognizable until the right moment.

This was the third time I had been out here, but I had to pretend I didn't know where I was going, and got confused at the Long Island Rail Road section of Penn Station, and in general put on a good dumb act about getting to Queens. Dad wasn't too smart about it himself, and I had to restrain myself from telling him which way to go. Sabine was the one who found the way to the right train—Sabine, who had hardly traveled at all in her life. I was glad when Dad commented on how smart she was.

We were all nervous. Even though there was no real money, it's not every day that you drop off a suitcase at a phone booth to be picked up by an evil zombie master with a nasty temper. How long would it take her to realize it wasn't really money? And what would she do to us when she found out? She had absolutely no compunction about controlling and hurting people. Nasty surprises were one of her specialties.

But Dad was going along with this, and that made me proud. Even though he believed in one way that I had behaved like an idiot, in another way he seemed to have gained more respect for me. He actually seemed more nervous than Sabine and I, clasping and unclasping the briefcase, chewing his lip. It made sense that he would be more nervous. He was older, of course, but Sabine and I had been through a lot more scary experiences than he had.

It seemed that we reached the station much sooner than the times I had been alone. And this time we had no trouble getting a taxi, maybe because the weather was good, and Dad was with us. Soon we saw the phone booth in the distance. We had the cab stop two blocks away from it.

Dad walked slowly toward it. Sabine and I took turns watching with the binoculars. The other one kept the camera focused on the phone booth. It was empty. She had said I would be waiting in it. Now we were as tense as Dad had been.

Dad arrived at the phone booth. He looked around, seeming confused.

And then someone walked out from behind a hedge next to the phone booth and started to hug Dad. It was my zombie, my enslaved soul.

Dad couldn't help it. He backed away and turned in our direction.

I had the bottle with my trapped soul in my backpack. "Open it now!" Sabine said. "Hurry!"

We started running toward the booth. At the same time, I had to get the bottle out of the backpack and try to unscrew it. The screw top was tight. "I can't open it!" I said, panting.

"Then just break it!" Sabine said, as we approached the booth.

Finally Dad was catching on. He put the briefcase in the booth and hugged the thing that looked like me.

Sabine had the camera and I had the tape recorder slung around my neck, the perfume bottle in my hand. I smashed it to the sidewalk so hard that some of the shards of glass burst up into the air and one of them cut my hand. A drop of blood appeared. I had never been so happy to bleed.

At the same instant the thing that was hugging Dad drifted away from him in my direction, and merged into me. I felt the same tingly sensation as when I had first found the bottle.

Dad grabbed the briefcase and then just stood there, looking more confused than ever.

That was when, as we had hoped so much that she would, Cheri Buttercup lost it. She stomped out from behind the hedge from which my image had appeared. She was wearing a fur coat on this warm day, and a lot of necklaces, and her face looked older in the sunlight than it had in her dark apartment. Sabine snapped several pictures as we reached her.

"What? You got *out*?" Cheri Buttercup cried, she was so shocked to see me. I got it on tape. Sabine was still snapping pictures, Dad holding the briefcase standing next to Cheri Buttercup.

Then she realized she'd blown it. She pretended to stagger. "Oh, excuse me, whoever you are," she said weakly. "Sometimes I have these little spells, and forget where I am." She put her hand to her forehead. "What am I doing here? Who are you people? I've got to get home and take my pills." She turned and started to totter away as fast as she could in her alligator-skin high heels.

"Stop!" Sabine said. "We have evidence now."

Cheri Buttercup turned back for an instant, her face distorted by rage. But she wasn't stupid, and she had gained control of herself. She turned and kept on going as fast as she could, *away* from the direction of her apartment. She wasn't giving away where she lived, even though she knew I knew. Maybe she hoped I'd forgotten.

She was also reaching for something in her leather handbag—some device or amulet that might call up other astral zombie slaves to fend us off. Sabine and I started after her.

And then two men in suits got out of a parked car just as she hurried past it. There was no way she could outrun them. They had her in a minute.

And we had the photos and the tape recording. She was finished.

I loved it when they snapped the handcuffs around her wrists. Not the kind of jewelry she was used to wearing. "Is this really necessary?" she snarled at them.

"Our orders, ma'am," one of the cops said.

"And it *is* necessary," Sabine said, breathing hard. "She probably has something in her purse she could have used to take care of all of us. You'd better take it, just to be sure."

One of the cops held out his hand. "Your bag please, ma'am."

She couldn't get it off her shoulder because of the handcuffs. Sabine whipped out a Swiss Army knife and started to slice through the leather strap. Cheri Buttercup tried to sidle away from her but the cops held her tightly.

Sabine finished cutting the bag and handed it to the cop. Cheri Buttercup tried to punch Sabine, even in her handcuffs, but the cops held her back. "And why the hell didn't he take care of *you*, you little interfering bitch," she screamed at Sabine. "If it weren't for you, I'd be . . . I'd have—" And then she snapped her mouth shut. "I'm not saying another word until I have my lawyer."

"Certainly, ma'am. That's the law," one of the cops said politely. "It's also the law that you have to come with us now." He turned to us. "And the rest of you, too, please. We have another car."

We didn't ride downtown to the station with Cheri Buttercup, which was probably just as well. "You have to be sure not to let her out on bail," Sabine said to the cop driving our car. "If she can get back to her apartment, she can escape from custody forever. Did you see what happened? When there were two Kens? And then one of them just merged into the real one?"

"Yeah, I saw," he said, shaking his head. "We'll have to talk about it at the station."

And we did. Three cops had seen the impossible. They confiscated her bag and found all sorts of weird amulets and strange devices in it. Cheri Buttercup was fuming, and later, when her lawyer showed up—a man with a huge gut and shiny, pointy shoes—he tried to argue that it was illegal not to set bail. The lawyer for the prosecution argued that this was an unprecedented case and it would not be safe to let her go. The look she gave us as they led her to her cell was worse than 3-D projectile-vomiting special effects.

Mom and Dad believed now, after what Dad had seen. But they had still not forgiven me. I had gotten involved with this extremely dangerous person because of my own bad judgment. The rules for my being grounded held.

But I didn't care. What I cared about was that, in the end, we had won.

But the most important thing was that I never would have met Sabine if I hadn't gone to see Cheri Buttercup. Having her hide my soul and become invulnerable was what had made me want to go to St. Calao, and that had changed my life—forever, I hoped.

We cried at the airport. We both knew that e-mailing is never enough, even instant messaging. But I was determined that I would see Sabine again, that I would be with her always, despite everything.

I had won before and I would win again.

sixteen

I wasn't a good enough writer to convey in an e-mail the expression on Cheri Buttercup's face when she got life. She was looking directly at me in the courtroom. It was scary. She would have used astral zombies to kill Sabine and me for sure, if she'd had access to any of her tools. It was very lucky the cops had seen the other Ken merge into me.

Sabine's doing, of course—she had timed it right, when she told me to smash the bottle and let the remaining part of my soul out. The fact that three cops and Dad had seen the merging take place had ruined Cheri Buttercup.

Meanwhile, Sabine wrote to me how she had alerted the *houngans* on St. Calao that the zombie slave of a *bokor* in New York was somewhere on the island—that was the only way Cheri Buttercup could have found out about Sabine and repeatedly tried to make me kill her. All the *houngans* together arranged a special ritual, with more drums and spirit possession than usual—*bokors* were their enemies, and they didn't want a *bokor* slave among them. The island was small, and Cheri Buttercup's zombie slave was drawn to the ritual. Since the bottle with the zombie's soul in it was not on St. Calao, the *houngans* had to perform a special, secret ritual—Sabine could not even describe it to me in an e-mail—to bind the zombie until it could be freed. I wondered if Cheri Buttercup could feel the loss of it in her prison cell.

Adams did beat me up once, and it hurt a lot when he broke my collarbone, but I survived it, and after that he left me alone.

It was almost good in a way, because the other kids could see I was normal again. It took a while, but gradually they began to for-get—or not so much forget as ignore—that brief period during which I had inexplicably beaten Adams. I slowly began to have friends again.

But I was still living for the summer. I wanted to go to St. Calao as soon as school was out. Sabine said that before I did, we had something more important to take care of—freeing all the souls imprisoned in bottles in the cave in Lake Wannamaka. Because the *houngans* wanted her to do this, they would see to it that her father was taken care of, and that she could get time off from work again—summer was the low season, anyway.

Sabine and I hugged each other at the airport tighter than ever. We were together again, and this time we were free. It was the best moment of my life.

"I feel like I've been looking forward to this forever," I said.

"Me, too," Sabine said. "But I'll feel even better when the job is really over."

Mom and Dad drove with us to the lake. We avoided the Hardings' place and stayed in a motel down the road. Mom and Dad had bought new diving gear for us so that Sabine didn't have to lug it on the plane. The lake was a different place in the summer, with sun glinting on the water, and families playing on the little beach near the pier, and speed boats, and jet-skis, as Mr. Harding had said.

And after we had finished with the bottles, Mr. and Mrs. Harding would be free, too.

And so here we were, swimming easily out to the island in the refreshing water, splashing each other and laughing, not going under until we reached the other side where the cave was. We had a big fishing net to carry the bottles in, as well as the flashlight and spear gun. It was much easier to see without the roof of ice, but the water was not perfectly clear like at St. Calao, and of course it would be dark inside the cave. Sabine had insisted on bringing a gun just in case Roger had freed himself from the wall.

And it was the thought of him that ended our goofing off. We slipped the breathing gear into our mouths and started going down. The water darkened around us as we descended, and I turned on the light. It felt almost effortless to get to the cave this time, because we had done it before under nearly impossible conditions.

Cheri Buttercup had one more surprise for us. Roger was gone and a new, larger guardian waited inside the cave of souls. The only explanation was that they must have allowed Cheri Buttercup to make a phone call, and she had called someone and told him or her how to replace the guardian—after all, her collection of souls was probably her most precious possession.

It was the man I had killed for Cheri Buttercup, powerfully built, a black belt in karate, not maimed and wounded like Roger had been. And we hadn't expected the guardian to lunge immediately—Roger hadn't done that. He went right for Sabine, so fast she didn't even have a chance to aim the spear gun. I would have screamed, but my mouth was full of rubber. The man slashed at her unprotected neck with the knife, with all the force he had.

Nothing happened.

The long sharp knife didn't go in. He tried again, and failed, just as the shark at St. Calao had tried twice to bite off my leg. He kept stabbing and stabbing uselessly. By this time Sabine, who seemed to be as strong as he was, had gotten it together to grab the spear and ram it into a crack in the wall through the chain, just like she had done to Roger. He was pinned to the wall now, helpless to stop us.

Sabine turned and looked at me. I couldn't read her expression. Her eyes were wide and she was breathing hard through the rubber tube.

We couldn't talk, but what was there to say? Suddenly all the little strange things about her fell into place. The way she had never been hurt, and could fight me off unlike anybody else, whether I had the pantyhose or not. Obviously the stockings had been a ruse, so I wouldn't know she was invulnerable. The way she had been so vehement, and spoken so harshly, about rescuing these souls.

The reason I had enjoyed kissing her, even in my zombie state, must have been because she was a zombie, too.

And most of all, the way she had seemed to risk her life repeatedly, and gone to such great lengths, supposedly just to help me. I had thought that meant she loved me so much. Now that fell away.

Did she even care about me at all?

She reached over to take my hand. I pushed it away. This was too much to deal with all at once. Anyway, we had work to do. Wasn't that why she had come here?

We laboriously began gathering up the bottles and putting them into the fishing net. Maybe it was a good thing we couldn't talk—it gave me time to think, instead of doing something rash.

Okay, Sabine was a zombie, whose master was someone on the

island who was an enemy of Cheri Buttercup, and had sent her here both times with the intention of destroying the New York *bokor*. Once that was done, the *houngans* could free Sabine. But maybe they wanted to keep her as she was, or Sabine didn't want to be freed.

She must be an astral zombie, because she didn't look dead like Roger and the man I had killed. Was I looking at her or was I looking at her soul? Was she really here or was she like the Hardings?

The fact that she hadn't told me, during all we had been through, felt at first like the ultimate betrayal. And I had felt so guilty so many times for putting her in danger, when she had never been in danger at all. I didn't see how I could ever forgive her.

But as we worked, side by side, I began to calm down. After all, she *had* saved me from Cheri Buttercup, whatever her ultimate motivation had been. The fact that she had kept her true nature a secret might not mean she didn't love me. Maybe it was a way of protecting me. After all, when I was a zombie, I had loved her—and she had really seemed to love me then, too, even knowing what I was.

Was it possible to love a zombie?

I put the last bottle into the fishing net. We still couldn't talk, but I reached out and took her hand. She squeezed mine, hard. Carrying the bottles, we ascended slowly, so I could decompress.

Enjoy this peek at William Sleator's novel

THE LAST UNIVERSE

u wont bleev what i overheard valerie say 2 jen," Lisa's
message was appearing in the instant message box. "i hardly
ever go 2 the mall, but i was in the bookstore and they were in
the next aisle, where the fashion magazines r. they didn't see
me. valerie sd she was worried about u, nobody ever saw u any
more, and—"

There was a knock on the door of my room. I groaned. It
could only mean one thing. I ignored the knock and just kept
reading.

"—and jen sd . . . well, maybe I better not say . . ."

"what did she say?" I wanted to know, typing fast.

The knock came again. "Susan," Mom said. "Gary wants to
go to the garden. He hasn't been out all day."

"Okay, I'll be right there," I said to Mom, feeling a little bit
frantic.

"they never wld have had this conversation if they knew i
could hear," Lisa's message was appearing. She was avoiding
my question.

"what did jen say?" I asked Lisa again.

"o . . . she sd u were acting funny 4 awhile."

I sighed. But I wasn't surprised, knowing what Valerie and Jen were like.

"and I found the coolest book. its all about how"

"sry, g2g," I wrote back. "gary wnts 2 go out."

"u don't want to hear about my new book?"

I could almost hear the hurt in Lisa's voice, and she was practically the only friend I had left. But what could I do? "i hv 2 tk hm out 2 the grdn, now. hes sick. he cnt walk," I wrote.

"y dont they get sombdy else 2 tk cr of hm?" Lisa wanted to know. "y duz it alwyz have 2 b u?"

"its like, they thnk its my duty," I wrote. "and he wants me 2, for some reason. and how can I rgu when hes sick?"

"Susan, please," Mom said, as she pushed open the door.

"by, lisa," I wrote. "ttyl. pos. sry. cya." I logged off without waiting for her to reply, hoping she would forgive me.

I turned around. Mom was looking sadly at me. "I know it's hard on you, too, Susan. But think of Gary."

"Okay, okay, sorry, I'm coming now," I said, standing up. At fourteen, I was taller than Mom; I was one of the tallest girls in my class. In one way it was a drag to be taller than most of the boys my age. In another way it was good to look older—because older boys were beginning to notice me. It was summer now, school had just gotten out, but I was already looking forward to high school next year, and the older guys. *And when I am back at school I won't have to spend so much time wheeling Gary around*, I thought, then felt guilty.

I followed Mom down the stairs. "And . . . and be pleasant to him, too," Mom said softly, as if Gary might hear us. "Try to make it fun for him. It's important. You don't know what it feels like to be . . . to be . . ." She took a deep breath. "To be going through what he is," she managed to say. In a minute she'd be crying.

"Okay, we'll have fun," I said. "I'll go right now." I wanted to get away before she broke into tears.

Gary was in his wheelchair in the kitchen, which is at the back of the house. He must have hated that wheelchair so much more than I did—he'd been in it for almost a month now. He'd been a great athlete, as well as a good student, good at everything—track, swimming, football—and now he was stuck in this chair. I never knew what to expect from him these days.

"The weather looks pretty good but it could change any minute," he said impatiently. "Come on, let's go."

I stifled my response to being ordered around by him. I knew he hated needing me.

Dad was proud of the plywood ramp he'd built over the short flight of steps from the back door, even though he was sad the whole time he was doing it, because of what it meant about Gary. If we didn't have this ramp, Gary wouldn't be able to go out at all. And now that he couldn't walk, Gary's favorite thing in the world was going out.

Out into the garden. The garden I'd always hated, and stayed out of as much as possible. But now, with Gary like this, I couldn't avoid it like before. It wasn't just the difficulty of pushing him around in the wheelchair over the uneven ground. It was the garden itself that was the disturbing part— the garden, and Gary, too.

If I wasn't so tall, I wouldn't have had to do this so much. But Mom had much more trouble with the wheelchair than I did. And what I had told Lisa was true. They all wanted *me* to be the one to wheel Gary around—especially Gary. He was sixteen, two years older than me, and before he got sick he hadn't wanted to spend any time with me at all. He'd always been doing sports, and at home he'd mostly ignored me, poring over his science books—he loved science. Now he wanted me to wheel him around as much as possible.

Was he punishing me?

I propped open the back door and took hold of the two rubber hand grips on the wheelchair. The ramp wasn't steep: Dad had made the slope as gentle as possible so it would be easy to negotiate, but the wheelchair still pulled me down it. I was always scared of losing control. I had to take small steps, pulling back on the handles as I went so slowly down. Every time, I wondered what would happen if I just let go of the chair.

Dad had inherited the property, which had been in his family for generations. That was why the garden was so big—land around here had been cheap when his great-grandparents had bought it. It had been farmland then, not the suburbs, but no one in the family had been a farmer who grew crops for money. Dad's great-grandparents had inherited some money and invested it in this land. Great-Uncle Arthur, who had also lived in the house, had been a scientist who won the Lebon Prize for quantum physics, for something about quantum mechanics. I had no idea what that meant. Everyone else in Dad's family had been businessmen. All of them, including Great-Uncle Arthur, the quantum scientist, loved to garden, for the pleasure of it, to create something they thought was beautiful.

Dad was an only child, and so the entire place had come to him. Neither he nor Mom cared much about gardening, but they had held onto the property for sentimental reasons; Dad knew that's what his parents—especially his father, whom he still seemed to miss—would have wanted. It wasn't just our ancestral home, it had been a kind of spiritual home to the family for generations, and Mom and Dad knew that. We wouldn't have been able to afford the taxes on all that land, except that Dad was an important real estate lawyer and knew how to wangle things downtown.

Still, before Gary got sick, Mom and Dad had started talking tentatively about selling a lot of the land; the garden was too big to keep up properly, and they could make a huge amount of money from it, and pay for college—for me, at least. Gary would have gotten sports scholarships. Both Dad's parents were dead now and would never have known. I had been so thrilled at the thought of people clearing the land, getting rid of the eerie old glades and rustling banks of shrubbery, and putting up neat houses with clean, open lawns. It would have been so great to have neighbors nearby.

But then Gary got sick, and suddenly he loved the garden so much. It was odd, because when he was well he hadn't cared all that much about it. He had never been afraid of it, the way I was, and he had enjoyed walking around in it, and playing hide and seek and war games with his friends when he was younger. Still, it had never been all *that* important to him.

But now that he was sick, the garden had become the center of his life.

Outside the back door was the lawn that surrounded our old two-story log house. Great-Uncle Arthur, one of Dad's more eccentric relatives, had removed the wooden siding to expose the original huge dark logs with mortar in between them. Even from here, the most open place, you couldn't see another house. The closest one was a half mile away, and Dad's family had made sure to plant thick borders of trees and dense shrubbery all around the perimeter of our land, so that we would have privacy and protection no matter what happened on the property next to ours. It had been smart of them—if you cared about stuff like that—to guess that the land around here would eventually get developed and wouldn't just stay open farmland forever. Apparently most people at that time didn't have as much foresight, and didn't imagine that this area would become a suburb of the city, full of houses with small yards, and malls and traffic.

But because they had planned so carefully, the ten acres behind our house felt completely secluded, especially the large section that bordered on the state park, which could never be developed. It would have been like being in the wilderness, except for the garden. Now that there were no more avid gardeners in the family, it was getting wilder and wilder. It was extravagant of Mom and Dad not to sell the land—a lot of developers wanted it. It was also extravagant of them to hire Luke, to do as much as one person could to take care of it, which wasn't a whole lot, since the garden was so big. But now that it was so important to Gary, they had no choice but to hold onto it.

"Which way do you want to go today?" I asked Gary, feeling apprehensive. It was up to him; he was the invalid. He could decide to go someplace ordinary, or someplace scary. I had noticed over the years that Gary, like me, had avoided the more eerie, distant parts next to the state park. Now he didn't seem to know the difference between what was scary and what wasn't, and wouldn't admit that he ever had.

"The pond," he said, looking straight ahead, almost as though he were talking to himself. "On a day like this, I want to go to the pond."

I hated the pond. The pond itself was small, and surrounded by tall, dense trees. Sun never seemed to go in there, and the water was always dark and gloomy.

Dad's aunt had drowned in the pond when she was five years

old. If that hadn't happened, and she had grown up and had her own family, the property would have been divided up, and our part would be a lot smaller. But my grandfather's younger sister had drowned, and the whole place had gone to him, and Great-Uncle Arthur, a bachelor. Then to Dad. I hated to think of that little girl going into the water and being pulled down, crying for help, and the pond so remote that no one could hear her. They didn't find her body for a whole day.

I had the feeling that the drowning wasn't the only bad thing that had happened in the garden. But Dad and Mom were closed-mouthed about anything else. We only knew about the aunt because of the old family pictures of her—it would have been impossible for them not to tell us what had happened to her.

"But it's not sunny today. Don't you want to go to someplace brighter?" I asked Gary, trying not to sound like I was begging.

"I feel like the pond," Gary said lightly, ignoring the pleading in my voice. And I knew that if I didn't take him there, he'd complain to Mom and Dad, and then I'd be in trouble. In trouble with my parents, and with Gary, too, and I didn't know which was worse.

I had never been a very assertive person. I usually did what other people, like the friends I used to hang out with, wanted to do. I preferred that to arguing.

I sighed, and began pushing the chair toward the path that led into the group of apple trees on the right. There were only about a dozen apple trees, but we had always called it the orchard. In the spring, the trees overflowed with white blossoms. Now the blossoms had fallen off and were brown and withering under the trees. The sun came out briefly from behind a cloud, and the bright green new leaves shimmered in the breeze, making dappled dancing shadows on the ground as

I pushed the wheelchair underneath them. And even though I hated entering this place, I could also feel how the apple trees might be beckoning, enticing.

"The apples from these trees are always the best," Gary said. "Better than any you can buy. Remember climbing up and picking them, Suze?"

I didn't remember Gary and I ever climbing the apple trees. Maybe he had done it with his friends, but not with me. I also didn't like the direction his words were taking, reminiscing about when he could walk, and climb. It could put him in a bad mood.

"They almost make me look forward to the fall, those apples," Gary said softly.

I pushed the wheelchair as quickly as I could over the grass, to get away from the apple trees. Mom and Dad didn't talk to me about what was wrong with Gary, but for several months he had been getting thin and weak, and now he couldn't walk. I didn't want him thinking about the fall and wondering if he'd see it. How could I distract him?

"Those apples are hard and bitter and have worms in them," I said. And then I didn't have to think of a way to distract him. I stopped the wheelchair suddenly. "Look at that!" I bent over so he could see me pointing, my heart thudding. "Those flowers around the outhouse!"

The wooden outhouse and the stone gardener's shed were past the orchard and to the left. The outhouse sat proudly behind the shed, on a slope of land that must have been manmade, it was so steep and abrupt in this flat place; stone steps were embedded in the grassy slope going up to it. Outhouses can be disgusting, but this one wasn't; it was neatly and solidly built, and always clean, with a bucket of lye and a dipper to sprinkle down the hole when you were done, so it never smelled bad. Not that I ever used it, or had even gone inside it in years.

Luke lived in the stone shed below it, which was full of tools, and he was the only one who used the outhouse. Luke was from someplace in Cambodia, some little town I could never remember the name of, where everybody probably had outhouses instead of real bathrooms anyway, so using the outhouse wouldn't matter to him.

Today, for the first time in my memory, brilliant red flowers on tall, two-foot-high stalks stood all around the outhouse. They had grown overnight.

"Don't be a dope," Gary said. "There's always been lots of stuff growing around the outhouse, because of what's underneath it."

"If I'm such a dope then I must be too stupid to find my way to the pond," I couldn't keep from saying. The sky was darker than before now. I gave a sharp tug on the wheelchair and Gary slipped forward slightly.

"You'll do what I want, Suze," he said, and smiled engagingly up at me, as if he wasn't scared by what I had just done. I knew he could tell Mom and Dad if I did anything mean to him; he knew I was in immediate control.

Hinges squeaked and Luke stepped out of the stone shed, carrying a shovel and rake, a trowel sticking out of the pocket of his overalls. His orange cat, Sro-dee, was perched on his shoulder. "Hello, Gary. Hello, Susan," Luke said. He was shorter than me, too, with dark skin, and black hair that fell over his forehead. When he smiled—he was always smiling—his dark eyes turned to slits.

"Those red flowers around the outhouse," I said to Luke. "They weren't there yesterday. How did they grow so fast?"

Luke turned and looked at them and shook his head, puzzled.

"Same flowers we have in my home, in the tropics," he said. "Never think they can grow here."

"Well, but did you plant them?" I pressed him. "Do they normally grow overnight?"

He shrugged. "I never plant them. Maybe the seeds fall out of my clothes or my shoes. Maybe they come from inside my body when I first came here and finally grow up from underneath. A mystery. And I think I know everything about this garden." He shook his head. "Well, I got work to do. Going to rain soon." He turned and walked away to the left, past the little hill with the outhouse on it, disappearing behind it.

I was mad at Gary for calling me a dope, and for ordering me around. It had felt good to shake the wheelchair.

"Please. Can we go to the pond before it rains?" Gary said.

I liked it that he was begging me. Maybe I didn't have to be afraid of what he would tell Mom and Dad. When we were alone together, I could do what I wanted.

My emotions about Gary changed from minute to minute. I resented him, I was often angry at him (though I had always avoided getting angry at people directly). But a lot of times I felt sorry for him, too.

I knew there were motorized wheelchairs; I'd seen people in them on the street. But of course they were much more expensive than this one, which the health insurance had provided. And Mom and Dad probably didn't think it was safe for Gary to be riding around all by himself. That left me to be the one to take him around most of the time. Great. It would have been different if he'd been friendlier to me before he got sick. But we'd never really been friends. And now he was my job.

I pushed the chair past the stone shed and to the right. Here there were banks of shrubs as tall as me, still in bloom, big round white and pale blue blossoms. Tall, scraggly weeds grew up among them now.

The raindrops started to fall when we were halfway down the row of shrubs, and then came a crack of thunder.

"No pond today, I guess," I said, feeling relieved not to have to go there—and also guiltily glad that Gary wasn't going to get what he wanted. "Have to hurry back before we get drenched."

Gary smiled up at me, looking handsome, like in the old days. "Rain won't kill us," he said.

"You think Mom would like it if I let you get soaked?" I asked him.

He couldn't argue about that. I turned the wheelchair around and pushed it back as quickly as I could, which wasn't very fast because it was so heavy and hard to steer, and the ground was so rough and uneven I had to keep pulling it back and turning it slightly and then pushing it forward again. Soon I was panting, and my arms were aching. Back past the row of shrubs, then the stone shed and underneath the apple trees, the wheelchair rocking, and across the lawn toward the dark old log house. I grunted with effort as I maneuvered it up the ramp.

And as I was struggling, Gary said, "We've got to get to the pond as soon as possible. Something's going to happen there and I want to be there when it does."